KB085296

아무도 돌아오지 않는 밤

아시아에서는 《바이링궐 에디션 한국 대표 소설》을 기획하여 한국의 우수한 문학을 주제별로 엄선해 국내외 독자들에게 소개합니다. 이 기획은 국내외 우수한 번역가들이 참여하여 원작의 품격을 최대한 살렸습니다. 문학을 통해 아시아의 정체성과 가치를 살피는 데 주력해 온 아시아는 한국인의 삶을 넓고 깊게 이해하는 데 이 기획이 기여하기를 기대합니다.

Asia Publishers presents some of the very best modern Korean literature to readers worldwide through its new Korean literature series 〈Bilingual Edition Modern Korean Literature〉. We are proud and happy to offer it in the most authoritative translation by renowned translators of Korean literature. We hope that this series helps to build solid bridges between citizens of the world and Koreans through a rich in-depth understanding of Korea.

바이링궐 에디션 한국 대표 소설 073

Bi-lingual Edition Modern Korean Literature 073

The Night Nobody Returns Home

김숨
아무도 돌아오지 않는 밤

Kim Soom

ASIA
PUBLISHERS

Contents

아무도 돌아오지 않는 밤

The Night Nobody Returns Home

1

구릿빛 양은들통에서는 한 무더기의 오리 뼈가 고아지고 있었다. 오리 뼈에서 우러난 누리끼리한 기름이 둥둥 엉겨 떠올라 장판지 같은 막을 만들어내는 동안, 거실과 부엌은 차차 어둠 속으로 가라앉았다. 부엌 맞은편 꼭 닫힌 방문이 소리 없이 열리더니, 노인이 걸어나왔다. 제자리걸음을 해 현관 쪽으로 돌아서더니 두 발을 질질 끌면서 움직여 갔다. 고개가 처들려서 있어서인가 노인의 몸은 마치 허공에 대롱대롱 매달린 듯 보이기도 했다. 현관문이 열리는가 싶더니, 한순간 노

1

A large quantity of duck bones was boiling in a big, copper-colored nickel silver pot. The blobs of yellowish duck fat oozing out of the bones kept rising up, covering the surface of the broth with a thickening membrane that looked like a sheet of oiled-floor-paper. Meanwhile, darkness began settling in the living room and the kitchen. The door of the room opposite the kitchen pushed open silently and an old man walked out. He marked time to turn toward the entrance hall, and started to shuffle across the living room. His head

인이 현관문 밖으로 지워지듯 사라졌다.

현관문이 저절로 닫히는 것과 거의 동시에, 영숙이 식탁 의자에서 쑥 몸을 일으켰다. 그녀는 부엌 형광등 스위치를 올렸다.

가스레인지 화력을 최대한 미약하게 줄여놓아, 들통 속 오리 뼈 국물은 뭉근하면서도 집요하게 고아지고 있었다. 하루하루 고요하고 끈덕지게 지속되는 노인의 일상처럼. 노인이 온종일 집 안에 틀어박혀 하는 일이란 오리 뼈를 고고, 전기문이나 성경을 필사(筆寫)하거나 티브이 뉴스를 시청하는 것뿐이었다. 날이 어둑해지면 노인은 슬그머니 방에서 나와 산책을 다녀왔다.

노인의 산책은 그다지 길지 않았다. 한 시간 정도, 고작 집 근처 골목들을 쏘다니다 돌아왔다. 집에서 그리 멀지 않은 곳에 근린공원이 있었지만, 그곳을 찾아가지는 않는 눈치였다. 영숙은 노인이 굳이 복잡하고 소란한 골목들을 헤매고 다니는 이유를 알았다. 쓸모가 거의 다해 버려진, 그러나 노인의 눈에는 아직 쓸모 있어 보이는 고물을 줍기 위해서일 것이었다. 노인은 기껏 주워온 고물을 누구에게도 내보이지 않고, 자신의 방 외짝 장롱 속에 차곡차곡 감추듯 쌓아두었다. 마치 그

was upturned; perhaps that was why his body seemed like it was dangling in the air. The old man opened the front door and disappeared behind the door as if he was erased out of existence.

The moment the front door was shut, Yeong-suk shot to her feet from out of her chair. She switched on the kitchen's fluorescent lamp.

The heat of the gas stove was set to minimum and the duck-bone broth in the pot simmered and thickened steadily, just like the old man's daily life had proceeded in silence and resolution. All he had done, cooped up in his house all day long, was make duck-bone broth, transcribe biographies or passages from the Bible, and watch TV. At dusk, he would sneak out of his room and go for walks.

The old man's walks were not long. An hour, perhaps? He had never ventured any farther than the alleys around where he lived. Not far from his house was a neighborhood park, but he didn't seem to visit that park at all. Yeong-suk understood why the old man felt compelled to wander around only the bustling, noisy alleyways: he probably wanted to pick up the things that people had tossed aside—things deemed still useful in his eyes. He hoarded them in neat piles in an odd

것들이 사후에 자신의 쪼그라들고 메마른 육신과 함께 땅 속에 파묻힐 귀중한 부장품이라도 되는 양. 선풍기, 액자, 시계, 화분 등등 낡고 찌그러지고 깨진 잡동사니들 속에 누워 영원히 잠든 노인의 모습을 머릿속으로 그려보던 그녀는, 어깨까지 떨면서 고개를 내둘렀다.

그녀는 현관 쪽을 흘끔 바라본 뒤, 국자로 들통 속을 휘저었다. 장판지가 찢기듯 기름이 엉겨 만들어진 막이 찢어졌다. 누리끼리하다 못해 푸르스름한 빛이 감도는 국물 위로 늑골과 목뼈, 엉치등뼈 등속이 삐죽삐죽 악다구니 치듯 올라왔다. 그녀는 국자로 뼈들을 꾹꾹 눌러 들통 바닥으로 가라앉힌 뒤, 국자 그득 오리 뼈 국물을 떴다. 국자 속 국물을 빤히 들여다보고 있으려니 저절로 노인의 눈동자가 떠올랐다. 타원형의 오목한 국자 속에 담겨 있어서인가, 노인의 흐려터진 눈동자가 국자 속에 그렁그렁 괴어 있는 것만 같았다. 자신을 빤히 응시하고 있는 것만 같아서 그녀는 국자를 들통 속에 내던지듯 처박았다.

노인은 오리 뼈들을 도대체 어디서 구해오는 걸까. 살을 싹 발라먹은, 자잘하고 앙상하다 못해 흉측하기까지 한 뼈들을.

wardrobe in his room, allowing no one to see them, as if those things would serve as precious burial accessories to bury alongside his shrunken, wizened corpse. Imagining the old man in eternal sleep, surrounded by worn-out, disfigured, shattered odds and ends—electric fans, picture frames, clocks, plant pots, and so forth—she shook her head from side to side and felt her shoulders trembling.

She threw a glance at the entrance hall and stirred the contents of the pot. Her stirring tore into the fatty layer on the broth's surface. Now it looked like shredded oiled-floor-paper. Competing for the surface of the yellowed, blue broth were things like ribs, neck-bones, and pelvic bones. She pushed the bones down to the bottom, and ladled the broth. As she stared into the broth in the ladle's bowl, she was reminded of the old man's eyes. Was it the oval shape of the ladle? His cloudy pupils seemed to be suspended like tears inside the broth. They stared her straight in the eyes. She threw the ladle into the pot.

Where did the old man get those duck bones? Those small, thin bones, completely stripped of flesh, grotesque.

'옥천오리식당'에서 얻어오는 것인지도 모르지…….

그녀가 그렇게 생각하는 데는 나름 그럴 만한 이유가
있었다. 작년 겨울, 그녀는 노인을 모시고 그 식당을 찾
아간 적이 있었다. 일흔셋 생일을 맞은 노인에게 오리
백숙을 사 먹이기 위해서였다. 마침 남편이 출장인데
다, 시누이마저 뭔 사정이 있어 며느리인 그녀 혼자 노
인의 생일을 챙겨야 했다. 아침에 미역국을 끓이기는
했지만 생일상을 차리기가 뭣해 노인을 모시고 그 식당
을 찾아간 것이었다. 그 식당을 알려준 이는 그녀의 친
정어머니였다. 믹서에 간 마(麻)를 넣고 삶은 오리백숙
이 밭솥만 한 항아리에 담겨 나오는데, 주말에는 꼭 예
약을 해야 할 정도로 유명하다고 했다. "10년 전인가 다
쓰러져가는 집을 개조해 식당을 냈는데 돈을 갈퀴로 긁
어모은다는구나. 오리백숙을 먹고 나면 찰밥이 대나무
소쿠리에 담겨 나오는데 그 밥이 또 그렇게나 맛있다."
평일인데도 자리가 없어 노인과 영숙은 다락 같은 곳에
올라가 오리백숙을 먹었다. 마를 갈아 넣어 풀처럼 끈
적끈적한 국물을 노인은 걸신들린 듯 떠먹어댔다. 낮게
내려앉은 천장을 떠받치듯 등허리를 너부죽이 구부리
고서. 노인 때문인지 몰라도, 그녀는 어쩐지 오리백숙

14

It might have been Okcheon Restaurant.

It was not just a wild guess; there was a good reason for her choice. Last winter, she took the old man to the restaurant on his 77th birthday to treat him to a dish of duck-boiled-with-rice. At the time, it so happened that her husband was away on a business trip and also her sister-in-law was unavailable. So as his daughter-in-law she had had to take care of his birthday celebration on her own. She cooked the customary seaweed soup in the morning, but didn't really feel like preparing many other foods for just the two of them. So she decided to take him to the restaurant. It was her mother who told her about the restaurant: They served a duck boiled with rice and ground yam in an earthenware pot as large as a rice cooker. The restaurant was so popular you had to make a reservation to eat there if you wanted to go on the weekend.

"About ten years ago, the owner renovated a run-down house on the present site and opened the restaurant. Now, he's busy counting the money that's rolling in. After the duck dish, they serve sweet rice in a bamboo basket, which is also absolutely delicious," her mother had explained.

It was a weekday, and yet no seats were avail-

이 못 먹을 음식처럼 역겨웠다. 반찬으로 나온 동치미 국물이나 떠먹다 찰밥을 미리 달라고 해 먹었다. 그런데 화장실에 다녀와 계산을 하려고 신용카드를 내미는 그녀에게, 식당 여자가 불쑥 물어왔다.

"친정아버지신가 시아버지신가, 오리백숙 좀 자주 사드려야겠어요."

"……?"

"글쎄, 오리 뼈를 얻을 수 있냐고 물으시네요."

식당 여자는 출입문 옆에 얌전히 서 있는 노인을 흘끔 바라보면서 말했다.

"오리…… 뼈를요?"

"그러게 말이에요."

"오리 뼈는 왜……?"

"왜는요? 그거라도 푹 고아 드시려고 그러시는 거겠지요."

식당 여자가 뻔하지 않느냐는 듯 말해 그녀는 몹시 당황스러웠다. 모욕을 당한 것만 같아 홱 돌아서서 식당을 나왔다.

그녀는 아무래도 노인이 그 식당에서 오리 뼈들을 구해오는 것만 같다. 오른쪽 눈썹 밑에 사마귀가 난 식당

able. So, in order to be served, Yeong-suk and her father-in-law had to climb up a flight of stairs into what seemed to be an attic. They sat at a table. The attic had such a low ceiling that it appeared as if the old man was trying to buttress it with his stooped back. When the food arrived, the old man began ladling the viscous, yam-infused broth into his mouth ravenously. Perhaps, the old man was the reason why she was now so disgusted by the duck dish. After she drank some pickled radish juice she asked for the sweet rice. After the meal, she briefly left the old man alone to use the wash-room. When she finally held out her credit card, the mistress of the restaurant asked out of no-where.

"Is he your father or father-in-law? You need to treat him to the duck dish more often."

Yeong-suk didn't know how to respond.

"Well, he just asked me if he could get duck bones from our restaurant."

As she spoke, Yeong-suk turned to face the old man standing docilely by the entrance.

"Duck bones?"

"Yes, duck bones."

"Why... duck bones?"

여자한테 구걸하듯 사정사정을 해가며…… 그렇지 않
고서야 사나흘마다 한 무더기나 되는 오리 뼈들을 어디
서 구해오겠는가.

　거실 시계는 7시를 막 지나고 있었다. 남편은 8시쯤
집에 돌아올 것이었다. 오후 4시쯤 남편으로부터 전화
가 걸려 왔을 때, 노인은 혼자 식탁에 앉아 오리 뼈 곤
국물을 떠먹고 있었다. 굵은소금만으로 간을 한 그 국
물을 노인은 시도 때도 없이, 그것이 마치 불로장생의
보약이라도 되는 양 떠먹었다. 저녁을 어떻게 할지 묻
는 그녀에게 남편은 집에 와서 먹겠다고 했다.
　밥과 국 다 아침에 먹고 남은 것이 있었다. 그녀는 냉
장고에서 먹을 만한 반찬들을 끄집어내 식탁 위에 늘어
놓았다. 반찬이라고 해야 어묵볶음과 오이소박이, 오징
어채볶음뿐이었다. 일주일도 더 전 반찬가게에서 산 오
이소박이는 짓물러 있었다. 노인만 아니면 남편과 지하
철역 근처에서 만나 칼국수나 한 그릇씩 사먹고 들어올
텐데…… 그녀는 매콤한 아귀찜이 먹고 싶기도 했다.
그녀는 귀찮았지만 자반고등어를 한 마리 굽고, 계란을

"He plans to boil them and drink the broth, of course."

The mistress of the restaurant put it in such a matter-of-fact way that she'd felt mortified. She spun around and walked briskly out the restaurant.

Something told her that the old man had gotten the duck bones from that restaurant in the end, though. He must have begged the mistress, the one with the mole under her right eyebrow. Otherwise, where on earth did he get a mountain of duck bones every three or four days?

It was just past seven according to the clock in the living room. Her husband was supposed to be back by eight. When her husband called at around four in the afternoon, the old man was drinking the duck-bone soup with a spoon alone at the dining room table. The old man flavored the soup with nothing but coarse salt and drank it throughout the day as if it was the elixir of life. When she asked her husband about dinner, he told her that he would have it at home.

Both the rice and soup were leftovers from breakfast. She took out several side dishes, which still looked okay, and set them on the table. They

네 알 풀어 대충 계란말이를 만들었다. 바지락은커녕 감자와 파도 넣지 않고 끓인 시금치된장국을 데웠다. 그녀가 그렇게 저녁식탁을 차리는 동안에도 들통에서는 오리 뼈가 쉬지 않고 고아지고 있었다. 오리 뼈 고는 냄새와 자반고등어 튀기는 냄새가 뒤섞여 부엌뿐 아니라 집 전체에 떠돌았다. 베란다와 욕실에까지.

30분이나 서 있었을까? 그녀는 두 다리와 발이 붓는 것을 느꼈다. 발가락들이 수족관 속 개불처럼 부풀어 오르는 것만 같았다. 그녀는 식탁 의자에 비스듬히 엉덩이를 걸치고 앉아 가빠오는 숨을 골랐다. 그녀는 임신 7개월이었다. 임신 5개월 때, 의사는 사내아이임을 그녀에게 슬쩍 알려주었다. 그즈음 남편이 마침 출장 중이어서 그녀는 시아버지인 노인에게 그 사실을 가장 먼저 알려주었다. 노인에게 아들이라고는 달랑 남편뿐이었다. 정작 노인 자신도 형제가 누이들뿐 대대로 아들이 귀한 집안이었다. 노인이 당연히 손녀보다는 손자를 바라리라는 것이 그녀의 생각이었다. 내심 안도하고 흐뭇해하겠지, 대를 이어줄 손자가 아닌가.

"아들이라지 뭐예요."

"……?"

were nothing special, just some stir-fried fish cakes, stuffed cucumber kimchi, and shredded, fried cuttlefish. The cucumber kimchi, which had been bought more than a week ago from a side dish vendor, was now soggy. If it were not for the old man, they could have just had a bowl of hand-made noodles or something near the subway station. She also felt like a dish of steamed anglerfish.

Reluctantly, she now grilled some salted mackerel, cracked four eggs and made an omelet. She also reheated the spinach bean paste soup made with neither surf clams nor potatoes nor green onions. Even as she set the dinner table, the cauldron of duck-bone soup simmered away on the stove. The mixture of smells from the salted mackerel and the duck-bone soup spread throughout the house, even to the balcony and the washroom.

She stayed on her feet for about another half hour. She felt her legs and feet swell. Her toes were swollen like spoon worms in a fish tank. She sat down obliquely on one of the dining room chairs and tried to get her breath back. She was seven months pregnant. Five months into the pregnancy, her doctor had told her that it was a boy. At the time, her husband was on a business

"제 뱃속의 아이 말이에요."

"그러냐……."

노인은 그 말뿐이었다. 아무리 무덤덤한 양반이래도, 어떻게 그렇게나 무덤덤할 수 있을까. 남의 집 며느리가 임신을 한 것도 아니고…… 여태 먹어보라면서 변변한 과일 하나 사다준 적 있던가. 그녀의 배가 하루가 다르게 불러오는데도 노인은 예정일이 언제인지 단 한 번 그녀에게 물어오지 않았다. 하기는, 내가 입덧을 그렇게 해대는 데도 오리 뼈를 온종일 고아댔으니…… 그녀는 임신 4개월째까지 입덧을 심하게 했고, 그것이 오로지 오리 뼈 고는 냄새 때문이라고 믿었다. 그녀는 오리 뼈 고는 냄새가 진동하는 집에서 물 한 모금 제대로 목구멍으로 넘길 수 없었다. 오리 뼈 곤 국물을 하도 먹어대서인지 노인의 얼굴에 부옇게 살이 오르는 동안, 그녀는 쇠꼬챙이처럼 말라갔다. 숨 쉬는 것조차 힘겨워 친정에 가서 보름 동안 지내다오기까지 했다.

"홀시어머니 시집살이보다 홀시아버지 시집살이가 더하다더라."

결혼 전 친정엄마는 그런 이유로 남편을 딱히 마땅해하지 않았다.

trip, so her father-in-law was the first person who'd heard the news. Her husband was the old man's only son. The old man himself had had only sisters; sons were rare in the family. Naturally, she thought that the old man would prefer a grandson to a granddaughter. He'll be pleased and relieved now that his grandchild can carry on the family line, she'd thought.

"It's a boy, I was told."

The old man raised an eyebrow.

"I mean the baby inside me."

"I see," he'd said.

That was all. Yes, he was a reticent man. Still, how could he be so indifferent to the news? It wasn't someone else's daughter-in-law that's pregnant. Had he ever been considerate enough to even buy any fruit for me?

As time passed, her belly got bigger and bigger, but the old man never even asked her when she expected the baby. But why should that surprise her? After all, he was the person who had no qualms about boiling duck bones all day long while she was suffering from morning sickness.

She had a severe case of morning sickness until the forth month of pregnancy. She believed that it

"계원 중에 삼부아파트 사는 이 말이다. 둘째딸인가가 시집을 가서 홀시아버지를 모시고 살았는데 술주정에다 잔소리가 어찌나 심하던지 이혼까지 할 뻔했다더라. 도장까지 찍어 이혼장을 내밀어서야 남편이 시아버지를 요양원으로 보냈다지 뭐냐?"

그렇게나 꺼리고 우려하는 친정어머니를, 그녀는 노인이 술 한잔 할 줄 모르는 단정하고 과묵한 분이라는 말로 안심시켰다. 그러나 결혼 2년 만에 노인은 그녀에게 도무지 속을 알 수 없는 의뭉스러운 노인네로 바뀌어 있었다.

"엄마, 천 길 물속은 알아도 한 길 사람 속은 모른다는 말이 왜 있는지 알겠어요."

"속담이고 뭐고 옛말들 중에 틀린 말이 하나 있는 줄 아냐?"

"그러게 말이에요."

"살면 살수록 흘려들었던 옛말이 뼈에 못처럼 박힐 거다. 옛말들이 죄다 뼈에 박혀 피 같은 녹물을 뚝뚝 흘릴 때쯤에야 철이 드는 게지. 혹 아냐? 정말로 접시 물에 코를 박고 죽은 사람이 정말로 있었는지도."

"노인네가 수박 한 통, 아니 주먹만 한 참외라도 하나

was all because of the smell of that duck-bone soup. Stuck in a house that reeked of boiling duck bones, she couldn't even swallow a mouthful of water. As the old man's face seemed to swell and droop with flesh, she seemed to be becoming as thin as an iron skewer, perhaps thanks to that duck-bone soup. When she had difficulty breathing, she went to her parents' home and stayed there for half a month.

"They say that living with a widowed father-in-law is more difficult than living with a widowed mother-in-law," her mother had said.

That was the reason why her mother hadn't readily approved of her marriage with her present husband.

"You know the person in my mutual loan group, who lives in Sambu Apartment Complex, don't you? Was it her second daughter? Anyway, one of her daughters got married and the couple lived with the husband's widowed father. The old man was a drunkard and such a nagger at that. The couple almost divorced. Only when the wife presented a signed divorce application form to her husband did he take his father to a home.

At the time, she reassured her very reluctant

사다줬어도 이렇게까지 밉지는 않겠어요."

친정에서 지내는 내내 그녀는 입덧으로 인한 스트레스를 노인의 흉을 뜯는 것으로 풀었다. 그녀가 친정에서 겨우 입덧을 가라앉히고 돌아왔을 때 집은 벽지까지 오리 뼈 고는 냄새에 찌들어 있었다. 그릇과 수저 행주 수세미에까지. 들통에서는 오리 뼈가 고아지고 있었고, 노인은 방에 틀어박혀 필사를 하느라 내다보지도 않았다. 그녀가 짐을 챙겨 친정에 갈 때만 해도 간디 전기문을 필사하고 있더니, 톨스토이 전기문을 필사하고 있었다. 초등학교도 마치지 못한 노인네가 간디를 알면 얼마나, 톨스토이를 알면 얼마나 알겠는가. 글씨쓰기 연습을 하는 것도 아니고 궁색스럽게 밤낮으로 뭘 그렇게 베껴 써대는가. 그러고 보니 노인이 한권 한권 필사 중인 전기문들도 길에서 주워온 것이었다. 어느 날 밤 스무 권 가까이 되는 전기문 전집을 주워 와서는 거실에 늘어놓고 걸레로 먼지를 훔쳤다. 얼마나 오래되었는지 누런 종잇장 위로 흰 벌레가 기어 다니고 군데군데 곰팡이가 피어 있었다.

노인네가 돌아올 때가 되었는데…… 오늘은 또 뭘 주워들고 돌아오려나?

mother by saying that her father-in-law-to-be was a man of few words and upright character. Now, however, two years later, her father-in-law had become a person whom she felt she would never understand.

"Mom, my father-in-law really brings the old saying home to me: It's easier to fathom the deepest waters than a man's heart."

"Old sayings are never wrong, didn't you know?"

"True."

"As you grow older, you'll see. The old sayings that you had no ear to before will hit home like nails impaling your bones. By the time all those nails in your bones have begun to rust, that's when you begin to understand life. Who knows? There might have been someone who drowned in a dishful of water."

"If he had bought me just one watermelon, no, just a tiny melon, then I wouldn't think of him as such an odious man."

While she stayed at her parents' place, she released the stress of morning sickness by backbiting the old man. When her morning sickness finally subsided, she returned home to find the entire place, including the wallpaper, bowls, spoons and

2

8시가 넘었지만, 남편은 집에 돌아오지 않고 있었다. 밤 산책을 나간 노인도. 남편은 그렇다 쳐도 노인은 돌아올 때가 지났다. 노인이 집을 나간 지 어느새 한 시간도 더 지난 것이다.

남편은 약속한 시간보다 귀가가 늦는 일이 잦았다. 무턱대고 두세 시간 늦는 경우도 종종 있었다. 남편은 잉크를 전문으로 만드는 회사의 영업사원이었고, 이런저런 술자리가 느닷없이 생기고는 했다. 이틀 전에도 남편은 아무리 늦어도 9시까지는 집에 오겠다고 해놓고 자정이 가까워서야 술에 취해 돌아왔다.

바싹 구워진 고등어를 접시에 옮겨 담는데, 계단을 올라오는 발소리가 들렸다. 그리고 빌라 어느 집인가, 현관문이 열리고 닫히는 소리가 들렸다. 그녀는 고등어가 담긴 접시를 식탁에 내려놓았다.

202호 여자가 돌아왔나?

그녀는 시금치된장국을 올려놓은 가스레인지 불을 껐다. 거무스름하게 짓물러진 시금치들이 누런 된장국물 속에서 혓바닥처럼 날름댔다. 그녀는 시금치를 한

chopsticks, and even dishtowels and pot scourer, reeking of duck-bone broth. The pot of duck bones was still boiling, and the old man hadn't even peeped out of his room, so busy was he transcribing. When she left for her parents,' he was transcribing the biography of Mahatma Gandhi. It was now the biography of Leo Tolstoy he was copying. How much could he, with less than an elementary school education, understand of Gandhi or Tolstoy? It couldn't be that he was practicing his penmanship. What, then, was he doing, pathetically transcribing all day and night? Come to think of it, all those biographies that the old man transcribed one after another were the ones he collected from the alleys. One night, the old man brought home some twenty-volume set of biographical works, spread them all over the living room, and wiped the dust off the books with a rag. The yellowed papers, the white worms crawling on them, and the blots of fungi here and there showed how old the books were.

It was time for the old man to come back home. What would he bring home tonight?

가닥 젓가락으로 건져 입으로 가져갔다. 질식시킬 듯 혀에 감기는 시금치를 겨우 식도로 삼키고 거실 시계를 쳐다보았다.

사실 그녀는 남편과 노인을 기다리기도 했지만, 202호 여자를 기다리기도 했다. 빌라 계단에서 몇 번 얼굴을 마주친 것 말고는 말 한 마디 섞어본 적 없는 그 여자를. 그녀가 그 여자를 기다리는 것은, 전날 노인으로부터 황당한 소리를 들었기 때문이었다.

"아래층 여자가 내일 저녁에 30만 원을 가져올 거다."

아래층이라면 202호였다.

"내가 그 여자한테 30만 원을 빌려주었다. 그 돈을 너한테 갚으라고 했다."

"저한테요……?"

"내일 저녁에 그 돈을 갚겠다고 했다."

"그렇지만 왜 저한테……?"

"꼭 갚겠다고 했으니…… 그래 꼭…….."

"……."

"그 돈을 받거든 너 쓰고 싶은데 써라."

노인은 그리고 산책을 나갔다. 노인네가 202호 여자를 보면 얼마나 봤다고 30만 원을 다 빌려주었는가. 그

2

It was past eight in the evening, but her husband hadn't been back home. Putting thoughts of her husband aside, the woman considered the fact the old man had gone out for a night walk and should have returned home already. He had left home over an hour before.

Her husband often came home later than the time he said he would. Sometimes he was two or three hours late without letting her know. He was an employee in the sales department of an ink manufacturing company, so alcoholic outings turned up unexpectedly and he had to attend. A couple of days before, he promised that he would be back by nine at the latest, but he had come home drunk close to midnight.

As she transferred the crisply grilled mackerel onto a plate, she heard footsteps coming up the stairs and then the front door of some condo unit in the building opened and shut. She placed the mackerel plate on the table.

Was it the woman in Unit 202?

She turned off the gas stove on which she had warmed the spinach bean paste soup. The dark,

녀는 그런 생각이 들면서도 공돈 30만 원이 생겼다는
생각에 은근슬쩍 기분이 좋았다. 그렇지 않아도 임신한
뒤로 다달이 적자였다. 매달 붓는 보험금에 적금, 공과
금을 제하고 나면 생활비가 빠듯했다. 지지난달에는 의
료보험 적용이 안 되는 양수검사를 받는 바람에 마이너
스통장까지 만들었다. 그런데 노인이 무슨 돈이 그렇게
나 있어서 202호 여자한테 30만 원을 다 빌려주었는가.
노인이 혹 남편 모르게 숨겨둔 돈이 있는 게 아닐까. 남
편이 딱히 그녀 몰래 용돈을 챙겨주는 것도 아닌데 노
인은 그럭저럭 잘 지냈다. 하긴 담배를 피우지도, 술을
마시지도 않으니 돈 들어갈 데가 별로 없을 것이었다.
놀러 다니는 걸 즐기는 노인도 아니었다. 친구도 별로
없는지 노인이 누구와 전화통화 하는 걸 그녀는 본 적
이 없었다. 수원에 살고 있는 딸과도 생전 전화통화 한
번 하지 않았다.

　30만 원을 덥석 꿔줄 만큼 노인이 평소에 202호 여자
와 잘 알고 지냈나? 그러나 노인의 성격으로 봐서 그럴
것 같지 않았다. 며느리인 나한테도 말 한 마디 건네는
적이 없는 노인네가 아닌가. 더구나 202호 여자는 직장
에 다니는지 낮에는 집에 없었다. 한 빌라에 살고 있다

soggy, tongue-like spinach pieces swirled in the yellowish soup. She fished up a piece of spinach with her chopsticks and placed the whole thing in her mouth. She managed to swallow the spinach that kept wrapping around her tongue as if to choke her, and then looked up at the living room clock.

In fact, she had been waiting for the woman who lived in Unit 202 as well as her husband and father-in-law. She had seen her several times in the building coming up and down the stairs. Other than that, she had never really talked to her. The only reason for her waiting for the woman was the outrageous thing the old man had told her the night before.

"The woman living in the unit below us will bring 300,000 *won* tomorrow evening."

The unit below us was Unit 202.

"I loaned 300,000 *won* to her. I told her to return it to you."

"To me?"

"She said she would pay it back tomorrow evening."

"But why to me?"

"She promised that she would pay it back... yes,

지만, 그녀는 202호 여자와 그다지 말을 나눈 적이 없었다. 40대 중후반으로, 남편과 두 딸과 함께 산다는 것 말고 아는 게 거의 없었다. 하긴 속을 도무지 알 수가 없으니……. 그녀는 어쩐지 노인이 빌라에 살고 있는 사람들에 대해 모르는 것이 없을 것만 같다. 그들이 어떻게 살아가고 있는지 속속들이 다 알고 있으면서, 모르는 척 의뭉을 떨고 있는 것만 같다.

노인은 심지어 내가 오리 뼈 곤 국물을 몰래 버린다는 것을 알면서도 모르는 척 시침을 떼고 있지 않은가. 내가 국자로 국물을 떠 개수대로 흘려버리는 것을 버젓이 목격해놓고도…… 그녀는 묘하고 엉뚱하게도, 노인이 그 사실을 아들인 남편에게 일러바치지 않는 것이 신경질 나고 견딜 수가 없었다. 노인이 모르는 척 시침을 떼는 것이 어디 그뿐인가. 노인이 먹다 남긴 밥과 국을 죄다 음식쓰레기통 속에 버린다는 것을, 노인이 벗어놓은 옷가지는 따로 분리해 세탁기에 돌린다는 것을, 노인이 쓰고 난 뒤면 왁스를 듬뿍 뿌려 좌변기를 닦아댄다는 것을 다 알면서도 모르는 척 시침을 떼는 것이다.

그녀는 새삼 노인이 자신의 집에 들어와 함께 산 지 2

definitely..."

She didn't know what else to say.

"Once you receive it, you can use it in whatever way you want to."

After saying so, the old man went for a walk. Why on earth had he loaned 300,000 *won* to the woman living in Unit 202 when he probably didn't know her well enough? Nonetheless, she felt good secretly thinking about the windfall. As a matter of fact, their family budget was always in the red after she'd gotten pregnant. Money always became tight after the monthly installment savings and utility bills. Two months back, the bank balance was minus because she had had the amniotic fluid test done, which was not covered by the health insurance plan.

Where had he gotten the money to lend to the woman living in Unit 202, and as much as 300,000 *won* at that? Perhaps, he had some money stashed away behind her husband's back? Her husband clearly wasn't secretly giving him any pocket money; and yet, he was getting by. In fact, he neither smoked nor drank, so he needn't really spend money. He was not the type who enjoyed outings, either. He seemed to have few friends. She had

년이 다 되어가고 있음을 상기했다. 잔병치레 없던 노인이 갑작스레 중풍으로 쓰러지는 바람에, 어쩔 수 없이 모시고 살게 된 것이다. 입원해 지내는 동안 빠르게 회복되기는 했지만, 노인의 말과 행동은 쓰러지기 전보다 어눌하고 굼떠져 있었다. 그때 남편은 노인이 혼자 살고 있던 빌라를 처분해 주식과 펀드에 투자했고, 투자한 지 8개월 만에 거의 날려버렸다. 그렇지 않아도 펀드가 한창 유행일 때였다. 서둘러 파느라 시세보다 3,4백만 원이나 밑지고 팔아넘긴 그 빌라는, 노인의 전 재산이나 마찬가지였다. 싫든 좋든, 그녀는 노인과 한집에서 살 수밖에 없었다.

그녀는 불현듯 어깨를 흠칫 경직시키면서 뒤를 돌아다보았다. 노인이 등 뒤에서 자신을 빤히 쳐다보고 있는 것만 같은 착각이 들어서였다. 그녀는 낮잠을 자다가도 버르적 깨어나고는 했다. 노인이 자신을 빤히 내려다보고 있는 것만 같아서였다. 설거지를 하다가도, 청소기를 돌리다가도, 베란다에서 빨래를 널다가도, 텔레비전이나 신문을 보다가도 흘끔…….

그녀에게 그런 버릇이 생긴 데는 다 그만한 이유가 있었다.

never seen him call anybody, not even his daughter in Suwon.

Was he on such friendly terms with her that he could readily lend her that much money? It seemed highly unlikely considering his personality. After all, he never talked to her, his own daughter-in-law. Moreover, the woman in Unit 202 seemed to have a job judging by the fact that she was never home during the day. Although they lived in the same condo building, they had never had any decent conversation. All she knew about the woman in Unit 202 was that she was in her mid- or late forties and lived with her husband and two daughters. 'Well, what do I really know about the old man, anyway?' For some reason, she felt that the old man knew everything about the people living in that building. Perhaps, he knew every detail of their lives, yet pretended ignorance.

The old man, in fact, must have known that she was throwing away the duck-bone broth he made, and yet he acted as if he didn't know. He had definitely seen her ladling out the broth and pouring it down the kitchen sink. Strange to say, what made her so upset was none other than the fact that the old man had never told his son on her. That was

노인이 들어와 산 지 1년이 다 되어가던 어느 날이었다. 그날도 남편은 8시쯤 집에 돌아오겠다고 해놓고는 9시가 넘도록 돌아오지 않고 있었다. 그녀는 하는 수 없이 노인과 단 둘이 식탁에 마주앉아 저녁을 먹었다. 그녀가 문득 고개를 들었을 때, 노인이 그녀를 빤히 쳐다보고 있었다.

"왜 그러세요……?"

"……."

"절 왜 그렇게……."

"……."

"절 왜 그렇게 바라보시는 거냐고요?"

　노인은 그러나 입을 꾹 다문 채 그녀를 빤히 쳐다보기만 할 뿐이었다. 노인이 딱히 해코지를 한 것도 아닌데, 그녀는 낯설고 이상한 공포심에 사로잡혔다. 딱히 뭐라고 설명할 길 없는.

　어쨌든 그런 일이 있은 뒤로, 그녀는 절대로 노인과 단둘이는 식사를 하지 않았다. 남편이 늦는 날이면 식탁을 차려놓고 방으로 들어가 버렸다. 노인이 식사를 다 마친 뒤에야 방에서 나와 혼자 식사를 했다. 노인도 혼자 식사하는 것이 편한 듯 식사를 다 마치면 자신의

not the only thing he pretended to be unaware of: he knew that she dumped all the leftover rice and soup from his meals in the garbage can. That she washed his clothes separately. That she wiped the toilet seat using plenty of disinfectant whenever he finished using the washroom. He pretended that he had absolutely no knowledge of any of this.

She was reminded that the old man had moved in with her and her husband almost two years before. He had been healthy until the day he suffered a stroke and the couple had no choice but to have him move in with them. While he was in hospital, he recovered quickly. Nevertheless, his speech and movement became inarticulate and slower than before.

Her husband sold the condo where the old man had lived alone, and invested the money in the stocks and funds only to lose all of it eight months later. It was at the peak of the funds craze. Her husband undersold the old man's condo in a rush and lost three, four million *won* over the sale. The condo was all the old man had. Whether she liked it or not, there was no way the old man couldn't live with them.

All of a sudden, she stiffened her shoulders and

방으로 조용히 들어가 버렸다. 그리고 그녀가 식사를 다 마칠 때까지 절대로 방에서 나오지 않았다. 남편이 어쩌다 일찍 퇴근해 돌아오는 저녁에나 노인과 한 식탁에 둘러앉아 아무렇지도 않은 듯 식사했다.

눈에 띄게 호전되기는 했지만, 노인은 아직 중풍 환자였다. 오리 뼈 국물을 떠먹을 때 숟가락을 쥔 노인의 오른손이 떨리는 것을 그녀는 여러 번 보았다. 오른손이 하도 떨려서 기껏 떠올린 숟가락 안의 오리 뼈 국물이 줄줄 옆으로 새는 것도 보았다. 다만 그것을 그녀가 모르는 척할 뿐이었다. 김이 무럭무럭 피어오르는 들통에서 오리 뼈 국물을 한 국자 한 국자 떠올리는 것이, 노인에게는 크고 무거운 벽돌을 한장 한장 들어 올리는 것만큼 힘에 부치는 일이리라. 그럼에도 그녀는 단 한 번 오리 뼈 국물을 떠 노인 앞에 놓아준 적이 없었다.

노인이 또 쓰러지기라도 하면 어쩌는가. 설마 갓난아이에다 중풍으로 쓰러진 노인 병수발까지 하게 되는 건 아니겠지.

그런데 202호 여자는 왜 돈을 갚으러 오지 않는 것이지? 설마 30만 원을 갚아야 한다는 것을 깜박한 것은 아닐까. 그녀는 30만 원이 노인이 아니라 자신이 꿔준 돈

looked around. She felt like the old man was staring at her from behind. Even in the middle of a nap, she would wake up, startled by the sense that the old man was staring down on her. Whether she was washing dishes, vacuuming, hanging laundry in the verandah, reading newspapers, or watching the TV, she would habitually look around to check.

There was a good motive that forced her into such a habit.

About a year after the old man moved in with the young couple, one day, her husband was supposed to be back home around eight in the evening, but instead he was over an hour late, as usual. She had to eat dinner with the old man, just the two of them, face to face. At one point, she looked up and realized the old man was staring at her.

"What is it?"

"..."

"Something's wrong with me?"

"..."

"Why are you staring at me?"

The old man just sat there staring at her, his mouth clasped shut. He wasn't doing anything particularly threatening, but she was overwhelmed by an unfamiliar and inexplicable fear. She didn't know

이라도 되는 듯 초조해졌다.

나한테 갚으라고 했으니 내 돈이지, 내 돈!

그녀는 30만 원을 어디에다 쓸지 미리 생각해두기까지 했다. 태어날 아이의 기저귀와 옷을 넣어둘 서랍장을 살 생각이었다. 30만 원이면 그럭저럭 쓸 만한 서랍장을 살 수 있을 것이었다.

거실 시계는 그새 9시가 다 되어가고 있었다. 다들 집으로 돌아갈 시간에 혼자서 골목을 헤매고 다닐 노인을 생각하니, 그녀는 저절로 미간이 찡그려졌다. 한 달 전쯤 그녀는 미장원에 다녀오다, 집 근처 골목을 홀로 걷고 있는 노인을 본 적이 있었다. 하필이면 노인의 뒷모습을……. 다세대주택들이 빽빽하게 들어선 골목이었다. 대문마다 쓰레기가 쌓여 있고, 전선줄들이 그물처럼 하늘을 뒤덮고 있는.

그날 그녀는 처녀 때부터 길러온 머리카락을 단발로 잘랐다. 머리카락에 반했다고 남편이 말했을 정도로 그녀의 머리카락은 길고 찰랑거렸다. 빗으려는데, 구역질이 나도록 머리카락에서 누린내가 났다. 오리 뼈 곤 국

what to think of it.

Anyway, from that evening on, she absolutely re-fused to eat with him alone. Whenever her hus-band was late, she would set the table for the man and go into her room. After the old man finished eating, she would come out and eat alone. The old man seemed to like that arrangement and, after his meal, he would quietly retreat to his room and stay there until she was done. Once in a while, when her husband returned home early, she would sit down at the table with her husband and the old man, feigning nonchalance.

The old man's recovery was well advanced; nonetheless he still showed signs of palsy. Many times, she saw his right hand shaking as he spooned up the duck-bone broth. His hand shook so bad that the broth would rain back into the bowl. But she pretended not to see. It had to be painful for the old man to spoon the broth from the large, steaming pot, one ladleful after another. As arduous as lifting up bricks one by one. But she had never brought a single bowl of broth to his ta-ble.

What if he collapsed again? Wouldn't she have to take care of the bed-bound palsy patient and the

물에 푹 담갔다가 꺼내기라도 한 것처럼. 그녀는 참을 수가 없었고, 곧장 지갑을 챙겨들고는 미장원을 찾아갔다. 머리카락이 싹둑싹둑 잘려나가는 동안 그녀는 거울을 빤히 바라보면서 노인을 원망했다. 생각해보면 머리카락을 자른 것이 오로지 노인 때문만은, 머리카락에까지 밴 오리 뼈 고는 냄새 때문만은 아닌데도 그랬다. 날이 더워지면서 그녀는 그렇지 않아도 길고 숱진 머리카락 때문에 갑갑함을 느꼈다. 부른 배 때문에 쪼그려 앉을 수도 없어 머리카락을 감는 것이 여간 힘든 일이 아니었다. 아직 아이를 낳지도 않았는데, 전보다 머리카락이 부쩍 많이 빠지는 것 같았다. 미장원에서 나와 그 옆 분식점에서 열무국수를 한 그릇 사먹고 돌아오는 길에 그녀는 노인을 보았다.

노인은 간장에 졸인 우엉 같은 골목을 두 발을 질질 끌면서 걸어가고 있었다. 노라도 젓듯 왼팔을 허우적거리면서. 과장되게 휘저어대는 왼팔과 달리, 40도 정도 허공으로 들린 오른팔은 의수처럼 뻣뻣하게 굳어 있었다. 노인은 성급히 발을 내딛었고, 그녀는 노인이 저러다 앞으로 꼬꾸라지지 않을까 조마조마했다. 두 발을 부단히 엇갈려 내딛는데도 보폭이 짧아서인지 노인의

newly born at the same time?

And while on the topic of the old man and his difficulties, why wasn't the woman in Unit 202 coming to return the money? Perhaps, she'd forgotten all about paying back 300,000 *won*?

She felt impatient, as if it was her, not the old man, who had loaned the money to the woman in the first place.

Well, he'd told her to return it to me. So, no matter what, the money was hers. Hers!

She had already thought about what to do with the money: she would buy clothes for the baby and a chest of drawers. 300,000 *won* could buy a decent chest of drawers.

The living room clock showed almost nine already. Despite it all, the thought of the old man wandering alone in the alleys when everyone was hurrying home made her frown. About a month before, she was on her way back home from a beauty parlor when she spotted the old man walking alone in an alley near their home. It was, worse luck, the sight of his back that she had caught. It was an alley lined densely with multi-family houses, heaps of garbage in front of each house and

걸음은 한없이 느렸다. 대여섯 발짝 거리를 두고 천천히 뒤따라 걷던 그녀는, 갑갑함을 느끼다 못해 결국 걸음을 빨리해 못 본 척 노인을 휙 지나쳐버렸다. 골목 끝에 거의 이르러 그녀가 슬쩍 뒤를 돌아다보았을 때 노인은 온데간데없이 사라지고 없었다. 눈을 휘둥그레 뜨고 골목 구석구석을 살폈지만 노인은 어디에도 없었다. 그녀는 노인이 그 골목에서뿐만 아니라 세상 그 어디서도 홀연히 사라져버린 것만 같아 한참을 멍하니 서 있었다. 그러나 그녀가 집에 돌아온 지 20분쯤 지나 노인은 아무렇지도 않게 선풍기를 주워들고 돌아왔다.

틀림없이 날 봤을 거야, 시아버지인 자신을 생판 모르는 남인 듯 지나쳐가는 날 말이지…… 노인네가 속으로는 날 얼마나 괘씸하게 생각했을까…….

아무튼 그날 이후로 그녀는 노인이 산책을 나간 동안 가능하면 집에 있었다. 혹시라도 집 밖에 나갔다가 골목에서 노인과 마주칠까봐서였다. 된장찌개에 넣을 두부를 사기 위해 빌라 계단을 내려가다 도로 올라온 적도 있었다. 그녀는 호박만 잔뜩 썰어 넣고 두부를 넣지 않은 된장찌개를 저녁식탁에 올렸다.

electrical wires crisscrossing the sky like a net.

That day, she'd gotten her hair cut short. She hadn't had a haircut since her maidenhood. Her hair had been so long and shiny that her husband told her that he was smitten by her hair when they first met. Earlier that day, though, she was just about to comb her hair when she realized her hair reeked of the duck-bone broth, as if she had washed her hair in it. She couldn't stand it any more, so she grabbed her purse and went to the beauty parlor. While her hair was being snipped short, she looked at herself in the mirror and blamed the old man.

Although, on second thought, it wasn't just because of the old man that she'd decided to get a haircut. As the weather was getting hotter, she found her long, thick hair troublesome. Since she couldn't squat down because of her swollen belly, she had great deal of trouble washing her hair. Even before giving birth, she was losing so much hair. She left the parlor and had a bowl of radish-kimchi noodle in the eatery next to the parlor. On the way back home, she saw the old man.

The old man was shuffling down the alley that looked like a long piece of burdock boiled down in

남편과 노인이 돌아오지 않는 동안 자반고등어는 딱딱하게 굳어갔다. 계란말이는 비린내를 풍겼다. 그녀는 밥솥에서 밥을 뜨다가 도로 쏟았다. 밥이 아니라 다른 걸 먹고 싶었다. 그렇지 않아도 그녀는 부쩍 식욕이 왕성했다. 입덧을 하느라 통 먹지 못했던 음식을 뒤늦게 보충하려는 듯 그녀의 몸은 끊임없이 먹을 걸 요구했다. 오늘 점심때는 중국음식점을 찾아가 혼자서 자장면을 다 사 먹었다. 노인이 혼자 식탁에 우두커니 앉아 오리 뼈 곤 국물을 숟가락으로 떠먹고 있을 시간에, 그녀는 기름지고 검은 면을 젓가락으로 건져먹었다. 그녀는 혹시나 해서 냉장고 안을 살폈다. 며칠 전 먹다가 남긴, 비닐봉지에 싸놓은 떡볶이가 그녀의 눈에 들어왔다. 그녀는 싱크대에서 냄비를 꺼내 봉지 속 떡볶이를 쏟았다. 떡은 차갑게 굳어 있었다. 그녀는 물을 조금 붓고 냄비를 가스레인지에 올렸다. 뚜껑을 꼭 닫아두었는데도 들통에서 새나오는 김이 자꾸만 그녀의 얼굴을 삼켰다.

언젠가 저놈의 들통을 내다버리든가 해야지…… 오리 뼈가 고아지는 동안 가스레인지가 내뿜는, 그리고 우러날 대로 우러난 국물이 내뿜는 열기는 대단했다. 본격적으로 더위가 시작되면 집은 가스레인지 위 저 들

soy sauce. He was swinging his left arm as if he was rowing a boat. Unlike the exaggerated swinging of the left arm, his right arm, raised in the air at about 40-degree angle, looked as stiff as a prosthetic arm. The man seemed to make careless steps, and she was afraid that he might fall down. He kept sticking out one foot after the other, and yet his pace was painfully slow. She walked slowly, five or six steps behind him, but soon she became impatient. She finally quickened her pace and walked past him, pretending that she hadn't recognized him. When she reached the end of the alley, she took a quick look over her shoulder. But now the old man was nowhere to be seen.

Her eyes widened and she began to retrace her steps. She looked in every nook and corner of the alley. She stood there for a long while without knowing what else to do. The old man seemed to have disappeared not only into thin air from this alley, but from the whole world. About 20 minutes after she arrived home, however, she saw the old man strolling back carrying an electric fan he had picked up along the way.

He must have seen her—his own daughter-in-law passing by him as if he was a stranger. How

통이 온종일 뿜어대는 열기로 들끓을 것이다. 더구나 앞뒤로 빌라 건물들이 꽉꽉 들어차, 바람이 제대로 들이치지 않는 집이 아닌가. 오리 뼈가 아니라, 내 뼈가 흐물흐물 녹아내리지나 않으면 다행일걸!

그녀는 기껏 데운 떡볶이를 먹는 둥 마는 둥 젓가락을 내려놓았다. 며칠 냉장고에 처박아두어서인지 맛이 나지 않았다.

깜박했으면 어쩌지? 그렇지만 꼭 갚겠다고 했다지 않았나, 꼭 갚겠다고, 꼭…….

그녀는 라면이라도 끓여먹을까 하다 202호에 다녀오기 위해 현관문을 나섰다. 202호 여자가 깜박했을 수도 있지 않은가. 202호까지는 302호인 그녀의 집에서 열두 계단만 내려가면 되었다. 그녀는 부른 배를 한 손으로 감싸고 계단을 조심조심 내려갔다. 발을 잘못 내딛어 계단을 굴러 떨어지기라도 하면 큰일이었다. 그녀가 202호를 찾아가는 것은 그것이 처음이었다.

그녀가 현관문을 다섯 차례나 두드렸는데도 안에서는 아무 대꾸가 없었다. 202호 여자는 아무래도 아직 돌아오지 않은 모양이었다. 그녀의 남편과 딸 또한.

그녀는 어쩔 수 없이 202호 현관문에서 돌아서서 다

insolent he must have thought she was!

After that day, she'd tried to stay home while the old man went out for his walks. One day, she started to go down the stairs thinking that she would buy some tofu for some bean paste stew, only to remember the old man and then returned home hurriedly. On the dinner table that day was a pot of bean paste stew full of zucchini, but with no tofu in it.

While she was waiting for her husband and father-in-law, the grilled mackerel hardened solid. The omelet began to stink. She tried to scoop out some rice from the rice cooker, but she dumped it back into the cooker. She wanted to eat something else. She had had an enormous appetite lately. Her body constantly craved things as if to compensate for what it had missed out because of her morning sickness. For lunch, she had gone to a Chinese restaurant alone and had eaten a bowl of noodles in black bean sauce. While the old man sat all alone at the table and drank the duck-bone broth one spoonful after another, she was busy eating the black, greasy noodles.

Now she opened the refrigerator and looked in-

시 계단을 올라갔다.

3

10시가 다 되도록 노인은 돌아오지 않고 있었다. 남편도, 그리고 202호 여자도. 아무도 돌아오지 않아서 그녀는 식탁을 치울 수도, 맘 편히 잠들 수도 없었다.

노인은 지금 어느 골목을 헤매고 있는가. 설마 집으로 돌아오는 골목을 잊어버린 건 아니겠지.

남편은 일부러 집에 돌아오지 않는 것인지 몰랐다. 그러니까 노인 때문에, 노인과 쓸데없이 마주치지 않으려고. 노인이 죽은 듯이 잠들기를 기다리느라 돌아오지 않고 있는 것인지도. 곰곰이 생각해보니 노인이 돈을 내놓으라고 요구하고 나선 뒤부터, 남편의 귀가가 늦는 날이 잦아졌다. 8시나 9시쯤 돌아오겠다고 해놓고, 노인이 잠든 뒤에야 술에 취해서는 돌아오는 날들이……

노인은 정말 입때껏 모르고 있었던 걸까. 그것 또한 다 알면서 모르는 척 시치미를 떼고 있었던 것이 아닐까. 만약 그렇다면 어떻게 여태까지 원망 한 마디 안 할

side to see if there was anything she liked. She found some rice cakes with hot seasoning wrapped in a plastic bag, leftover from a couple of days ago. She put a small pot in the kitchen sink and emptied the bag into the pot. The rice cake pieces were hardened and cold. She poured some water to the pot and put it on the gas stove. Even with the lid on tight, the steam from the great pot of simmering duck-bone broth engulfed her.

One of these days, she'd throw that big pot away or something. While the duck bones boiled and simmered, the heat from the gas stove and the long simmered broth became intense. At the peak of the summer, the place would seethe with the heat emitted throughout the day from that big pot of simmering broth. The couple's condo building was located in between two rows of densely built condo buildings, so there was not much fresh air blowing in from the outside. I'm lucky if my bones won't melt down before the duck bones!

Although the rice cake had warmed up, she found it unsavory, perhaps because it was in the refrigerator for some days. She put her chopsticks down.

What if the woman in Unit 202 had forgotten all

수가 있을까. 아들이 달랑 남편뿐이라지만, 전 재산이던 빌라 판 돈을 노인과 한 마디 상의 없이 날려버렸는데도.

정말이지 뜬금없게도 노인이 그만 돈을 내놓으라고 요구해온 것은, 두 달쯤 전이었다. 그날 남편은 8시 전에 퇴근해 집에 돌아왔다. 그녀는 돼지고기 김치찌개를 끓여 저녁 식탁을 차렸다. 그녀가 따로 대접에 떠준 찌개 국물을 숟가락으로 떠먹다 말고 노인이 문득 남편에게 물어왔다.

"그래, 8천만 원이 틀림없지?"

남편도, 그녀도 도대체 무슨 뜻인지 몰라 노인을 물끄러미 바라보았다.

"다는 아니어도 된다. 다는 아니어도……."

노인은 중얼거리고 숟가락으로 건져 올린 김치쪼가리를 입으로 가져갔다.

"9천만 원을 다 줄 필요는 없지……."

입을 우물우물하다 말고 또다시 그렇게 중얼거렸다.

"4천만 원이면 충분할 것 같구나."

"4천만 원이라니요?"

남편이 그제야 젓가락을 식탁에 탁 내려놓고 노인에

about the money? But she promised that she would pay it back. The old man had told her so. He said she would definitely pay it back, definitely...

She thought about having some instant noodles, but soon changed her mind and left her home for Unit 202. The money might have slipped her mind. She needed to take only twelve steps down the stairs from her condo, Unit 302, to Unit 202. She took careful steps down, one hand protecting her belly. It would be a terrible accident if she slipped and fell. That was her first visit to Unit 202.

She knocked on the front door five times, but there was no answer. It seemed that the woman hadn't come back from work yet. Her husband and daughters weren't home, either.

She had no choice but to turn around and climb up the stairs.

3

It was past ten and the old man was not back home yet. Her husband and the woman in Unit 202 weren't back, either. She couldn't clear the dinner table yet, and she certainly didn't feel like she could get any sleep.

게 물었다.

"늙은 사람들끼리 모여 사는 아파트가 있다는구나."

"아파트요……?"

노인에게 그렇게 물은 사람은 남편이 아니라 그녀였다.

"실버타운이라고…… 3천만 원만 내면 당장이라도 입주를 할 수 있다지 뭐냐……."

노인은 남편과 그녀의 중간, 텅 빈 공간을 두 눈으로 더듬거렸다.

"날마다 운동도 시켜주고, 때마다 관광버스로 여행도 데리고 다닌다지 뭐냐. 상주하는 간호사도 있어서 약도 꼬박꼬박 챙겨준다니……. 여태 은행에 넣어두었으면 이자가 그럭저럭 붙었겠지."

노인은 그러니까 빌라 판 돈 8천만 원에서 4천만 원만 내놓으라는 소리를 하고 있는 것이었다. 남편은 8천만 원을 주식과 펀드에 투자하면서 노인에게는 은행에 적금으로 묶어놓았다고 안심시켜 놓았다.

"은행이자가 6프로라 쳐도 8천만 원이면 일 년에……."

"요즘 이자를 6프로까지 주는 은행이 어디 있대요?"

Which alley is the old man meandering along now? Did he forget which alley to take to come home?

Perhaps, her husband was not coming back on purpose. Maybe it was also because of the old man —her husband didn't want to face the old man either. He might very well be waiting for the old man to fall into a sleep as sound as death itself. Come to think of it, ever since the old man demanded his money her husband had begun to come home late more and more frequently. He would promise to come back eight or nine, but then return home drunk only after the old man went to bed.

Did that mean that the old man really didn't know until that day? Or did he pretend ignorance when he knew everything? If so, how did he manage to stay silent, without making any complaints? Maybe it was because her husband was the only son he had. But that seemed very unlikely if he knew that his son had lost all the money that he'd gotten from the sale of his condo, the only property he had.

It was about two months before when, out of the blue, the old man demanded his money back. Her husband came home early that day before eight. She cooked a pot of pork meat kimchi stew for

남편이 버럭 짜증을 냈다.

"8천만 원이 적은 돈도 아니고 도둑놈들이 아닌 이상에야 은행들이 그 정도 이자는 줘야 되는 거 아니냐."

"모르는 소리 좀 하지 마세요. 고작해야 3프로가 조금 넘는 게 요즘 은행 이자란 말이에요."

"8월 전에는 들어갔으면 싶다. 날이 아주 더워지기 전에 말이다. 날이 너무 더워지면 서로 불편하기만 하니……."

노인은 그리고 먼저 식탁에서 일어섰다. 평소보다 늦은 밤 산책을 나갔다. 그날 이후 노인은 더는 돈 얘기를 꺼내지 않았다. 그렇지만 언제 또 노인이 4천만 원을 내놓으라고 요구해올지 모른다는 게 그녀의 생각이었다. 워낙에 속을 알 수 없는 노인네이니……. 더구나 8월 전에는 들어갔으면 싶다고 못 박지 않았나. 그렇지만 4천만 원을 당장 어디서 구한단 말인가. 더구나 아이가 태어나면 돈 들어갈 곳 천지일 것이다. 친정엄마가 큰오빠네 아이들을 돌보고 있어서 산후조리원에 들어가 산후조리를 해야 할 형편이었다. 그녀는 8월 전까지 남편이 4천만 원을 노인의 손에 쥐어주지 못하리라는 것을 알았다. 게다가 출산예정일이 8월 초였다. 노인네도

dinner. While spooning up the stew that she served him in a separate bowl, he suddenly asked her husband.

"Yes, it was 80 million *won*, right?"

Neither her husband nor she knew what he was talking about, so the couple just stared at him.

"It doesn't have to be the whole amount, but..."

The old man mumbled. He picked up a piece of kimchi with his spoon.

"You don't need to give me the whole 90 million."

He mumbled again while chewing.

"40 million *won* would be enough."

"40 million *won*?" her husband finally asked, putting his chopsticks down with a clatter, "What do you mean?"

"They say that there's an apartment complex where old people live together."

"An apartment complex?"

It was she who'd asked the question, not her husband.

"It's called Silver Town... They say I can move in right away if I pay 30 million *won*."

The old man's eyes were groping somewhere in the space between her and her husband.

"They'll help me exercise everyday and take me

내가 아이를 낳기 전에 이 집에서 나가고 싶은 거겠지. 아무리 그래도 두 달 뒤면 태어날 손자에 대해 어쩌면 저다지도 무심할 수 있단 말인가, 남 손자도 아니고…….

노인만 없으면 저 방을 아이 방으로 꾸밀 수 있을 텐데…….

아이가 태어날 때가 가까워서인지, 그녀는 부쩍 노인이 차지한 작은 방을 아이 방으로 꾸미고 싶은 욕심이 생겼다. 전세로 살고 있는 빌라는 방이 고작 두 칸이었다. 큰방은 그녀 부부가, 작은 방은 노인이 쓰고 있었다. 노인이 들어오기 전까지 작은 방은 옷방으로 썼었다. 거실은 소파도 들여놓지 못할 만큼 좁았다. 아들이라고 했으니 파란색으로 벽지도 새로 바르고, 커튼도 달면 좋으련만…… 친구가 준다고 한 요람을 놔줄 곳도 마땅찮았다. 요람을 들여놓기 위해서는 큰방 침대를 버려야 할 판이었다.

임신했을 때 누군가를 미워하면, 뱃속 아이가 미워하는 그 누군가를 쏙 빼닮는다지……. 그녀는 노인을 닮은 아이가 태어나지 말라는 법이 없다는 것을 알았다. 아이에게는 친할아버지가 아닌가. 노인의 어수룩하게

on trips to places on a tour bus. There's a live-in nurse who takes care of our medications. If the money's been in a savings bond in the bank, the interest alone may be not too bad."

What the old man meant was that my husband might give him only 40 million *won* back out of 80 million. When her husband had invested the 80 million *won* in the stocks and funds, he'd reassured the old man by saying he had put the money in a bank as installment savings plan.

"With an interest rate of, say, 6%, the sum of 80 million will earn in a year..."

"What bank these days sets the interest rate at as high as 6%?"

Her husband's face turned red.

"80 million is not a small sum. Unless the banks are in the robbery business, shouldn't they give at least that much interest?"

"Oh please. You don't know anything. The bank interest is slightly over 3% these days."

"I'd like to move in before August, before the weather gets too hot. Hot weather will only make us all feel uncomfortable."

The old man left the table first and went for a walk later than usual. After the day, he had never

처진 눈매와 긴 인중을 빼닮은 아이가 태어나지 말라는 법이 어디 있는가. 그렇지 않아도 그녀는 요즘 들어 부쩍, 남편이 노인을 닮아도 지나치게 닮았다는 생각이 자주 들었다. 며느리인 나와는 피 한 방울 섞이지 않았다지만, 남편에게는 친아버지가 아닌가. 일찌감치 죽어 사진으로밖에는 본 적 없는 시어머니를 닮았다고 생각했는데 그게 아니었다. 아내인 자신에게까지 속내를 좀처럼 드러내지 않는 것마저 다 노인을 닮아서인 것만 같았다.

그녀는 거실로 가 전화기를 집어 들었다.

"엄마, 저예요."

"으응……."

"벌써 주무셨어요?"

"9시만 넘으면 그렇게 잠이 쏟아진다……."

"……."

"어떻게 네 시아버지는 잘 계시냐?"

언제부턴가 친정어머니는 그녀와 전화통화 할 때 노인의 안부를 가장 먼저 물어왔다. 임신한 뒤로 만성두통처럼 그녀를 괴롭히는 짜증과 울화의 근원이 시아버지인 노인이라는 것을 누구보다 빤히 알기 때문이었다.

brought up the subject again. However, she thought nobody would know when the old man might ask for the money again, since she had no idea what was going on in his head. Besides, he had already driven the nail in saying that he wanted to move out before August. Where would they get that kind of money right away?

Moreover, once the baby arrived, they would need so much money for miscellaneous expenses. Her mother was taking care of her elder brother's children at the moment, so she would have to stay in one of the post-delivery care centers. She knew that her husband would never be able to repay 40 million *won* to his father. To make matters worse, she was expecting in early August. The old man wanted to move out before she had the baby. Still, how could he be so indifferent to his own grandson, who was arriving in two months, as if it was someone else's?

If he moved out, though, she could prepare the room for the baby.

As the expected day approached, she had an ever-growing need to have the old man's room back and turn it into a nursery. There were only two rooms in their leased condo. The couple used the

"오늘도 오리 뼈 곤 국물을 한 주전자는 잡수셨을 거예요."

"그 노인네도 원, 백 살까지 살겠네……!"

"엄마, 괜히 그런 말 마세요. 말이 씨가 된다잖아요."

"너는 어떻게 먹는 건 잘 먹고?"

"시아버지가 온종일 집에 붙어 있어서 그런지 먹고 싶은 게 있어도 눈치가 보여 해먹을 수가 있어야지요. 온종일 감시당하는 것 같은 게 징역살이 하고 뭐가 다르겠어요. 양로원 같은 데라도 다니면 오죽 좋아요? 바둑 같은 거라도 두러 다니든가요."

"얘, 놔둬라, 놔둬…… 것도 다 성격이다."

20분 넘게 계속된 통화를 끝내고, 그녀는 노인이 쓰는 방에 들어와 있었다. 이삼 일에 한 번 청소기를 들고 그 방에 들기는 했지만, 그녀는 낯선 이의 방에 몰래 숨어든 것처럼 꺼려지고 불안했다. 세 평이나 될까? 방 안에 가구라고는 거울이 달린 외짝 장롱과 철제 책상, 텔레비전, 2단 서랍장이 전부였다. 아들 집으로 들어오면서 노인은 살림을 거의 다 버렸다. 노인만큼이나 오래

bigger room and the old man the other. Until the old man moved in, they'd used the smaller one as a clothes room. The living room was too small even to put a sofa in. It's a boy, so blue wallpaper and a curtain would be nice. There was no proper place for the crib that one of her friends was going to give her. In order to put the crib in, they would have to get rid of their own bed.

"If you hate someone while you are pregnant, the baby will be the spitting image of the person you hate." She'd heard that saying several times before and she realized that there was a good possibility her baby might resemble the old man, who was his grandfather, though. The baby might very well have its grandfather's innocent-looking, droopy eyes and the long groove of the upper lip. Recently, she'd become keenly aware that her husband bore too much resemblance to the old man. Yes, of course, it was only natural. She had no blood connection with the old man while her husband was his bio-logical son. And yet, at first she had thought that her husband took after her mother-in-law that she had never met except in pictures. But now, even her husband's reticence seemed to have come from the old man.

되고 고장 나 쓸 만한 살림이 워낙 없기도 했다.

옷걸이에 꿰어 벽에 걸어놓은 쥐색 잠바에 그녀의 시선이 저절로 갔다. 마치 노인의 혼이 쏙 빠져나가버리고, 그럴싸한 허울만 남아 벽에 매달려 있는 것만 같았다. 그도 그럴 것이 노인은 코디네이션 하듯, 잠바 밑에 검은 기지바지를 받쳐 걸어놓은 것이었다. 잠바 위에 베레모까지 슬쩍 걸쳐 놓아서일까? 그녀는 베레모를 들추면 노인의 뭉그러진 빨랫비누 같은 얼굴이 불쑥 튀어나올 것만 같았다. 그녀는 베레모를 들추고 싶은 충동을 억누르고 책상 쪽으로 움직여 갔다.

책상 위에는 노인이 필사 중인 성경책과 초등학생용의 칸칸이 널찍한 공책이 펼쳐져 있었다. 그새 스무 권도 넘는 전기문을 다 필사한 걸까. 노인이 성경을 필사하는 것은 종교심 때문이 아니리라. 노인은 신자가 아니었다. 신자가 아닐 뿐 아니라 노인에게는 이렇다 할 종교가 없었다. 신자가 아니면서 성경을 필사한다는 사실이 그녀는 어쩐지 우습고 괜한 수고만 같았다. 더구나 오리 뼈 곤 국물을 떠먹을 때조차 덜덜 떨리는 그 손으로 필사는 무슨…… 그러나 필사는 아무 하릴없는 노인에게 취미이자 소일거리이리라. 노인은 성경에 적

She went into the living room and picked up the phone.

"Mom, it's me."

"Oh..."

"Are you in bed already?"

"I can't stay up after nine in the evening."

"..."

"How is your father-in-law?"

For some time, her mother had inquired after her father-in-law first thing whenever she called. After she got pregnant, she constantly suffered from irritation and resentment and chronic headaches, and her mother knew well that the old man, her daughter's father-in-law, was the cause.

"Today alone, he probably had a kettleful of duck-bone broth."

"That old man, he'll live to be a hundred!"

"Mom, don't say that. You know what they say, words sow seeds."

"How about you? Are you eating well?"

"Father-In-Law stays home all day, so I can't even cook what I want to eat. I feel as though he's watching me all the time. It doesn't seem very different from being in jail. How wonderful would it be if he just spent some time at one of those cen-

힌 글자들을 그대로 한 자 한 자 공책에 옮겨 적으면서
자신에게 얼마 남지 않은 시간을 견디기라도 하는 걸까.
이 성경책도 틀림없이 골목 어디선가 주워온 거겠지.

그녀는 책상 밑으로 넣어놓은 의자를 꺼냈다. 그 위에
엉덩이를 반쯤 걸치고 앉았다. 노인이 공책에 옮겨 적
은 글자들을 한 자 한 자, 지워 없애듯 읽어 내려갔다.

무릇 의복과 무릇 가죽으로 만든 것과 무릇 염소털로
만든 것과 무릇 나무로 만든 것을 다 깨끗이 할지니라.

어찌나 꾹꾹 눌러썼는지 글자들은 노인이 손가락으
로 눌러 죽인 개미들만 같았다. 어지럽게 소용돌이치는
지문에 짓눌려 비명횡사한 개미들이 공책 위에 일렬횡
대로 나열되어 있는 것만 같았다. 줄과 간격을 또박또
박 맞추어서. 하지만 자세히 들여다보면 글자들은 한
획 한 획 가늘게 떨리고 있었다.

그녀는 몇 줄 건너 뛰어 계속해서 읽어 내려갔다.

ters for senior citizens? Or, if he'd play *Go*?"

"Please, leave him be. The lives people live are based off of their personalities."

Finally she hung up the phone after speaking with her mother for over twenty minutes and went into the old man's room. Every two or three days, she entered his room with her vacuum, but each time she felt uneasy, as if she were sneaking into some stranger's room. It was about four square yards. Or, maybe a bit smaller than that. There wasn't much furniture in the room. Except for an odd wardrobe, an iron desk, a TV set, and a chest of double-stack drawers, there was nothing else there. After he moved in with his son, he threw away most of his furniture and appliances that were as old and broken as the old man himself.

Her eyes drew to the dark gray jacket hung on the wall. The draped jacket made her imagine that only the old man's exterior self had been left there, decent-enough on the surface, yet deprived of its soul. The effect seemed to be doubled by the black trousers hanging from under the jacket, as if the old man had put them together as a coordinate. He had even casually placed a beret over the collar

금, 은, 동, 철과 상납과 납의 무릇 불에 견딜 만한 물
건은 불을 지나게 하라. 그리하면 깨끗하려니와 오히려
정결케 하는 물로 그것을 깨끗케 할 것이며 무릇 불에
견디지 못할 모든 것은 물을 지나게 할 것이니라.

한 자 한 자 소리 내어 읽어나가는 동안, 노인을 향한
실뿌리처럼 자잘하고 어수선하며 수십 가닥이던 감정
들이 뒤엉키고 비비 꼬여 한 가닥을 이뤘다.

굵고 분명해진 한 가닥의 감정.

그것은 뜻밖에도 미움이나 연민 같은 감정이 아니라
공포감이었다.

무서운 노인네지 뭐야…… 그녀는 스스로도 모르게
중얼거리고 고개를 오른쪽으로 돌렸다. 눈가에 바르르
경련이 일도록 베레모를 노려보았다. 그녀는 아무래도
벽에 걸린 베레모 속에 노인의 얼굴이 숨어 있는 것만
같은 생각이 강렬하게 들었다. 그녀는 의자에서 몸을
일으켰다. 베레모 쪽으로 한 발짝 한 발짝 조심스럽게
다가갔다. 베레모로 손을 뻗었다.

베레모를 확 밀쳐내는 동시에, 그녀는 자신도 모르게

of the jacket. She felt that if she lifted the beret, the old man's face would pop out—the face that looked like a crumbling bar of washing soap. Resisting the temptation to lift the beret, she moved on toward the desk.

On the table was a copy of the Bible that the old man was transcribing and an open, widely ruled notebook one would expect to see grade schoolers using. Had he finished copying all of the biographies, all of the twenty-odd volumes? Probably, he was not transcribing the Bible out of any sort of religious faith. He was not Christian, nor did he have any other religion. She found it rather ridiculous and useless for a non-Christian to transcribe the Bible. Especially for a person with a hand that trembled terribly, a hand he couldn't even use to spoon his duck-bone broth properly. Nevertheless, transcribing could be a hobby for the old man who otherwise had nothing to do. Was he trying to endure what little time he had left by copying the Bible letter by letter onto the notebook? He must have picked up the Bible from some alleyway, too.'

She pulled out the chair from under the desk. She sat on the edge of the chair and began to read the notebook, word by word as transferred by the

비명을 내질렀다. 베레모가 내던져지듯 방바닥으로 떨어졌다.

베레모 뒤에 감추어져 있던 것, 그것은 그저 못 대가리였다. 그런데도 그녀는 노인의 얼굴이 방 안 어딘가에 숨어 자신을 빤히 지켜보고 있는 것만 같은 기분을 좀처럼 떨쳐버릴 수 없었다. 베레모를 주워 제자리에 걸어둘 생각도 않고 그녀는 서둘러 노인의 방을 나왔다.

노인의 방문을 꼭 닫아둔 뒤, 그녀는 202호에 다녀왔다. 노인이 꿔주었다는 돈 30만 원을 받아오기 위해. 그렇다고 오늘 밤 안으로 반드시 30만 원을 받아내야 하는 건 아니었다. 그렇지만 그녀는 자꾸만 신경이 쓰였고, 오늘 밤 편히 잠들기 위해서라도 받아내는 게 낫겠다는 판단이 들었다. 그렇지 않아도 그녀는 산달이 가까워오면서 불면에 시달렸고 어젯밤만 해도 새벽 3시가 넘도록 잠을 이루지 못했다.

202호 여자는 아직 돌아오지 않았다. 그녀의 남편과 딸도. 매일 이렇게 늦는가? 202호 여자가 좀처럼 돌아오지 않고 있는 것에 대해, 그녀는 짜증을 넘어 분노를

old man, as if she was trying to erase them with her eyes.

And purify all your raiment, and all that is made of skins, and all work of goats' hair, and all things made of wood.

He had pressed his pen down so hard that the letters looked like ants flattened to death under his thumb. The dead ants, which had been caught off guard and crushed by the swirling fingerprint of the old man's finger, were carefully arranged on the pages of the notebook, horizontally, file by file, and meticulous spaced. However, a closer look revealed the fact that each stroke of the letters showed signs of the slightest tremor.

She skipped several lines and kept on reading.

Only the gold, and the silver, the brass, the iron, the tin, and the lead, everything that may abide the fire, ye shall make it go through the fire, and it shall be clean: nevertheless it shall be purified with the water of separation: and all that abideth not the fire ye shall make go through the water.

느꼈다. 오늘 밤 돈을 꼭 갚겠다고 했으면 갚아야 하는 것 아닌가. 그것도 아버지뻘일 노인의 돈을 꿔갔으면…… 그렇지만 202호 여자가 돌아오지 않는 데는 다 사정이 있을 것이었다.

아무도 돌아오지 않고 있어서인지, 그녀는 다른 이들은 집에 돌아왔는지 궁금해졌다. 다들 여느 날 밤처럼 아무렇지도 않게 돌아왔는지…….

그녀는 계단에 난 창문에 붙어 서서 앞 빌라를 살폈다. 앞 빌라는 그녀가 살고 있는 빌라와 열 발짝도 떨어져 있지 않았다. 4층 빌라였는데, 불이 켜진 창문이 하나도 없었다. 다들 돌아와 벌써 잠든 걸까? 아니면 다들 아직 돌아오지 않은 걸까? 노인과 남편, 그리고 202호 여자가 돌아오지 않은 것처럼.

그녀는 어쩌면 다들 돌아오지 않고 있는 것은 아닌가 하는 의심이 들었다. 그러니까 다들…….

As she read along one word after another, her feelings toward the old man, those confused and fragile feelings, began to weave into a solid strand.

This clear, almost concrete line of feeling, to her surprise, had nothing to do with either hatred or compassion. It was fear. Most definitely, fear!

"What a frightening old man!" she breathed aloud and turned her head to the right. She glared at the beret on the wall so intensely that the skin around her eyes twitched. She couldn't free herself from the nagging sense that the old man's face was hiding under the beret. She raised herself from the chair and began making carefully toward the beret.

She reached for it and slapped it off the hook, crying out in spite of herself. The beret fell to the floor.

There was nothing but a nail-head there. Still, she just knew that the old man's face was somewhere in the room watching her every move. Without bothering to return the beret back to its hook, she rushed out.

She closed the door tight behind her and then left home to visit Unit 202 to get back the 300,000 *won* the old man had loaned to her. As a matter of

4

11시가 다 되도록 돌아오지 않는 노인을 걱정하면서, 그녀는 한편으로는 노인이 돌아오지 않고 있는 것에 대해 안도하는 마음이 들었다. 솔직히, 노인이 산책을 위해 현관문을 나설 때마다 그녀는 노인이 돌아오지 않았으면 하고 바라곤 했던 것이다. 노인이 마땅히 갈 곳이 없다는 것을 알면서도 저대로 멀리 어디론가 가버렸으면 하고……. 한 달에 한 번 정도만 서로 얼굴을 보면서 살면 오죽 좋을까. 그래서인가 산책을 끝낸 노인이 스스로 현관문을 따고 들어설 때 그녀는 어쩔 수 없이 실망감에 사로잡히곤 했다. 노인의 손에 고물이라도 들려 있으면 울화가 치밀기까지 했다. 그렇지만 생전 딸집에도 다니러 가지 않는 노인이지 않은가. 지하철만 타면 갈 수 있는 딸집에도. 남편이 4천만 원을 해주지 않는 한 노인이 갈 만한 데라고는 양로원뿐이리라.

그녀는 노인이 당장이라도 집에 돌아와 4천만 원을 내놓으라고 요구해올 것만 같아 불안했다. 남편이 아닌 그녀에게.

노인이 얼마나 고집스러운가를 그녀는 누구보다 잘

fact, there was no dire need to get it back within the night. Nonetheless, she found herself constantly thinking about it, and made up her mind to have it returned even if it was only to help herself sleep peacefully that night. As her delivery date approached, she had already begun suffering from insomnia. Even the night before, she wasn't able to fall asleep until past three in the morning.

The woman in Unit 202 was not back yet. Neither was her husband nor her daughters. Were they always this late? The woman's failure to return home momentarily moved her from irritation to outright fury. If she promised to repay, then she had to keep her promise, not to mention the fact that she had borrowed the money from a man old enough to be her father. But the woman must have had her own reasons for failing to return.

Since no one seemed to be coming home, she suddenly wondered if the other families were back home safe and sound, like on any other night.

She stood close to the staircase window to look at the other condo building less than ten steps away from her own. The four-story building had no lit windows. Were they all sleeping? Or has no one returned home, yet? Like the old man, her

알고 있었다. 스스로의 의지나 의사라고는 전혀 없는 듯하지만, 노인은 스스로가 정해놓은 규칙대로 흐트러짐 없이 살아가고 있었다. 며느리인 그녀에게 일상을 의지하고 순종하는 척하지만, 물 위에 뜬 기름처럼 철저히 겉돌며. 내가 오리 뼈 고는 것을 그토록 질색하는데도 온종일 오리 뼈를 고아대는 노인네가 아닌가. 죽음을 떠올릴 수밖에 없는 영정사진을 거실 벽에 보란 듯이 걸어놓은 것만 봐도……. 자신의 죽음이 그다지 멀지 않았다는 걸 수시로 아들며느리에게 일깨워주려는 꿍꿍이속이었을까. 넉 달 전쯤 노인은 그녀와 한 마디 상의 없이 자신의 영정사진을 거실 벽에 걸어놓았다.

"아버님한테 저 영정사진 좀 떼라고 해요. 볼 때마다 섬뜩해 죽겠지 뭐예요. 꼭 죽은 사람을 보는 것만 같잖아요."

그녀는 질색을 하면서 남편에게 그 말을 대엿 번은 했다. 그러나 영정사진은 여전히 거실 벽에 걸려 있다. 그녀는 께름칙한 것뿐만 아니라 영정사진 속 노인의 옷차림마저 마음에 들지 않았다. 영정사진 속 노인이 말끔하게 차려입은 개량한복은 하필 그녀가 사준 것이었다. 그녀는 그것을 백화점 지하매장에서 70프로나

husband, and the woman living in Unit 202?'

She suspected all of them hadn't come home. Which meant all of them...'

4

On the one hand, she was worried about the old man. It was close to eleven in the evening and he was not yet back home. On the other hand, she felt relieved. To be honest, whenever the old man went for a walk she wished he wouldn't come back. She knew that he had no other place to go, and yet she hoped he would walk out the front door and just keep walking. It would have been so nice if they saw each other only once in a month. Whenever he marched back through the front door after one of his walks, she would inevitably feel an overwhelming sense of disappointment. If he was carrying a piece of junk, too, she would feel the anger boiling inside. The old man had never visited his own daughter who lived only a subway ride away. Unless her husband gave the 40 million to him, the only place he could go was a home for the elderly.

She was afraid that the old man would return

세일된 가격으로 샀다. 그녀는 일부러 가격표를 떼지 않고 노인에게 주었다. 싸게 사놓고도, 그 옷이 얼마나 비싼 옷인지를 노인에게 알려주기 위해. 그녀는 급기야 노인이 개량한복을 세일된 가격으로 샀다는 사실까지 다 알고 있을 것만 같은 의심이 들었다.

오리 뼈를 고지 말라고 말해야겠어, 노인네가 돌아오기만 하면…….

그렇지만 그녀로서는 202호 여자가 언제 돌아올지 알 수 없는 것처럼, 노인이 언제 돌아올는지 또한 알 수 없었다. 더구나 그녀의 집으로 들어와 사는 동안 노인의 귀가가 그렇게까지 늦은 적이 한 번도 없었다. 노인은 경조사나 볼일이 있어 외출했다가도 9시 전에는 어김없이 집으로 돌아왔다. 조용히 작은 방으로 들어가 여자가 잠들 때까지 가능한 나오지 않았다. 여자가 잠든 새벽에야 방에서 나와 몽유병자처럼 거실과 부엌을 어슬렁거렸다.

차라리 시아버지가 아니라 시어머니였더라면, 그랬더라면 살림과 아이를 맡기고 직장 일을 다시 할 수도 있을 것이다. 결혼과 동시에 넌덜머리가 난다면서 직장을 때려치웠지만, 그녀는 직장 생활이 그립기도 했다.

right then and demand to have the 40 million *won* back, demand it from her and not from her husband.

She knew better than anybody else how stubborn the old man was. He appeared to have no will or opinion of his own, but in fact, he lived his life faithfully abiding by the rules set only by himself. He pretended to be docile and dependent on her for his everyday life, but he had always kept some measure of separation between them, like oil separating itself from water. He was the kind of person who, knowing how much she hated his boiling duck bones, kept at it all day long.

Just look at that picture of his which was just bound to remind them of death! About four months earlier, the old man had hung his own funeral-portrait on the living room wall, discussing it with nobody. By hanging it there on the living room wall, in full view for everyone, he may have been plotting to remind them over and over of his own approaching death.

"Please tell him to take the funeral-portrait down. It's so creepy I feel as though I am looking at a dead person all day."

She had told her husband this several times. And

남편의 얼마 되지 않는 월급으로 언제 아파트를 장만하고, 남들처럼 아이를 키우겠는가. 그녀는 마음만 먹으면 취직이 아주 어렵지도 않을 것 같았다. 그녀는 중소 공장에서 경리 일을 했고, 결혼하고 나서도 다른 중소 공장으로부터 경리로 와달라는 제의를 받았다.

오늘 밤 안으로 돌아오겠지, 노인이 갈 데가 어디 있다고······.

남편은 4천만 원을 구하는 중일까. 그 많은 돈을 구하는 것도 쉽지 않겠지만, 덥석 구한다고 해도 문제였다. 빌리는 순간, 4천만 원은 고스란히 남편이 떠안아야 할 빚이 되어버리기 때문이었다. 갚아야 하는 빚으로 치자면 4천만 원은 너무나 큰 돈이었다. 4천만 원에 비해 턱없이 적은 돈이었지만, 그녀는 오늘 밤 안으로 어떻게든 202호 여자한테서 30만 원을 받아내야 한다는 강박이 들었다. 그 돈을 오늘 밤 안으로 받아내지 못하면 영영 못 받을 것만 같은 불안이 엄습하기까지 했다.

고약한 노인네, 이왕 줄 거면 직접 받아서 줄 것이지······.

그런데 노인네가 202호 여자에게 돈을 빌려주기는 준 것일까. 그녀는 아무래도 노인이 202호 여자에게 30

yet, the picture was still hanging on the wall. She felt uneasy not only about the picture itself, but about the clothes the old man wore in the picture. The old man in the picture was neatly dressed in none other than the reformed traditional costume she had bought for him. She'd bought it on a 70% sale in the basement outlet of a department store. She didn't take the price tag off when she handed it to the old man. Although she bought it at a bargain price, she wanted him to know how expensive it was. Now, she even suspected the old man had found out she'd bought it at a sale price.

"I should have told him not to boil duck bones. If he comes back, then..."

Her resolution notwithstanding, she didn't know when the old man would return, just as she didn't know when the woman in Unit 202 would come back. What's more, he was never late coming back as long as he'd lived with them; he was always back before nine and he would go into his room and stay there until she was sound asleep. It was only around dawn that he would reemerge and shuffle about the living room and kitchen.

If he was her mother-in-law, not father-in-law, then she could have a job outside, leaving the

만 원을 빌려주었다는 것이 이상하기만 했다. 그렇다고 빌려주지도 않고 빌려줬다고 할 양반은 아니지 않은가. 노인은 그렇다 쳐도, 아무리 급해도 윗집 사는 노인네 한테 돈을 다 빌릴까. 그녀는 자신 같으면 아무리 한 빌라에 살고 있는 노인이래도 30만원을 빌려달라는 소리가 선뜻 나오지 않았을 것만 같은 생각이 들었다. 202호 여자가 돌아오면 알겠지, 202호 여자가 돌아오기만 하면…….

그녀는 식탁을 치우려다 관두고 침대로 가서 누웠다.

잠결에 그녀는 현관문이 열리고 닫히는 둔중한 소리를 들었다. 그것은 분명히 현관문이 열리고 닫히는 소리였다. 그녀는 두 눈을 똑바로 뜨고 삼사 초 동안 꼼짝없이 누워 있다가 몸을 일으켰다. 202호 여자가 돌아온 게 아닐까. 그녀는 침대에서 몸을 일으켰다. 헝클어진 머리카락을 매만지고 거실로 나갔다. 시간은 어느새 자정이 가까워오고 있었다. 202호 여자가 돌아왔다고 해도 찾아가 돈을 받아내기에는 지나치게 늦은 시간이었다. 미안해하기는커녕, 날 이상한 여자로 생각하지나

housekeeping and children in her care. As soon as she got married, she quit her job saying that she was sick and tired of it. Then she realized that she missed it at times. With her husband's meager salaries, she didn't know when they could buy their own apartment and raise kids like other couples. She didn't think her getting a job would be too difficult. She had a work experience in an accounting section of a medium-scale factory. Even after her marriage, she'd been offered work as an accounting clerk in another medium-scale factory.

"He should be back by tonight. He doesn't have any other place to go."

She wondered if her husband was trying to get 40 million *won* somehow. It wouldn't be easy to get that much money, but even if he did, that wouldn't solve their problems. The minute he borrowed 40 million, it would become just another debt binding her husband. As a debt to repay with interest, 40 million was far too large a sum for the couple. Compared to it, 300,000 *won* was nothing. Nonetheless, she felt compelled to get it back from the woman in Unit 202. She even felt that if she failed to get it paid back tonight, she would never be able to.

않을까. 어서 돌아오기를 내가 이렇게나 애타게 기다렸다는 사실을, 그 여자가 알기나 할까. 돌아오지 않는 동안, 내가 그녀의 집을 두 번이나 찾아갔다는 것을.

그녀는 202호를 찾아가기 위해 현관문을 열고 복도로 나갔다. 현관문이 열리고 202호 여자의 남편이 고개를 내밀었다. 그녀는 당황스럽고 민망했지만, 이미 엎질러진 물이었다. 그녀가 윗집에 사는 여자라는 것을 깨닫고 그 남자는 의아한 표정을 지었다.

"무슨 일이세요?"

"아주머니 계세요."

"집사람 말입니까?"

남자의 눈이 조금 커졌다.

"네……."

"집사람은 왜……?"

"혹시 잊어버리셨나 해서요."

남자가 무슨 말이냐는 듯한 표정을 지었다.

"아주머니가 꿔간 돈을 꼭 갚겠다고 하셨다지 뭐예요, 꼭……."

그녀는 괜히 얼굴이 화끈거리고 배가 조금 당겼다.

"꿔간 돈이요?"

86

What an odious old man! If he wants to give it to me, he himself should get it from the woman and then give it to me.

But, had he really loaned money to the woman in Unit 202? She found it very odd that the old man had lent 300,000 *won* to the woman in Unit 202. 'Still, he wouldn't say he had loaned it if, in fact, he hadn't. He wasn't that type of person. What about the woman downstairs? No matter how urgent her need, how could she borrow the money from an old man living upstairs?' If she were the woman in Unit 202, she would have hard time asking the old man for a loan of 300,000 *won*, even if he was living in the same condo building. Well, she'd find it out once the woman came back home, once she was back in Unit 202.'

She was about to clear the table, but then she changed her mind and went to bed to lie down.

She awoke to the sound of a front door opening and closing heavily. It was definitely a front door. She lay still for a few seconds with her eyes wide open. Then she raised herself. Was it the woman in Unit 202? She got out of the bed, tidied her hair, and went into the living room. It was already close

그녀는 퍼뜩 202호 여자의 남편한테서라도 노인이 꿔준 돈을 받아내야겠다는 생각이 들었다. 그만큼 그 돈을 오늘 밤 안으로 어떻게든 받아내고 싶었다.

"저희 시아버지가 아주머니한테 30만 원을 빌려주셨나 봐요. 그 돈을 저한테 갚기로 했는데 아무리 기다려도……."

"그럴 리가요……. 여간해서는 남한테 돈을 꾸는 사람이 아닌데."

남자가 얼른 그녀의 말을 끊었다.

"아주머니는 아직 안 오셨나 봐요?"

"집사람이 돈을 꿨을 리가 없을 텐데……."

남자가 고개를 갸웃거렸다.

"저희 시아버지가 그러셨어요. 202호 아주머니가 30만 원을…… 아주머니는 아직……."

"집사람은……."

당황해하던 남자의 얼굴이 시멘트처럼 굳었다. 남자의 등 뒤에서 조용히 아빠, 하고 부르는 여자애의 목소리가 들려왔다.

"집사람은……."

남자는 한숨 끝에 입을 다물어버렸고 그녀를 2초간

to midnight. It was too late for her to go down to Unit 202 to get the money back even if the woman was back. Her neighbor might think she was crazy, rather than feeling apologetic. But could she even understand how anxiously she'd been waiting for her to get back? Would she realize that she'd visited her place twice already while she was out?'

She pushed the front door open and went out into the hallway to go down to Unit 202. The woman's husband opened the front door and poked his head out. She felt embarrassed but decided to face him. Realizing that she was from Unit 302, the man suddenly looked confused.

"What is it?"

"Is your wife home?"

"My wife, you mean?"

The man's eyes widened.

"Yes."

"What do you want to see my wife for?"

"I wonder if she's forgotten."

The man seemed to have no clue at all about what she was talking about.

"Your wife promised that she would definitely pay back the money she borrowed. Definitely..."

She blushed and felt her belly growing tight.

빤히 바라보다 현관문을 닫았다.

"저기⋯⋯."

그녀는 닫혀버린 현관문에 선뜻 돌아서지지가 않아 잠시 멍하니 서 있었다. 뭔가⋯⋯? 아직도 돌아오지 않았다는 것인가? 이렇게나 밤늦게 빚쟁이처럼 찾아온 것이 기분 나쁘기라도 한 것인가? 여간해서는 돈을 꾸지 않는 사람이라니, 그럼 노인이 거짓말이라도 한다는 것인가. 도대체 다들 언제야 돌아오려고, 여태까지 돌아오지 않고 있는 것인가.

그녀는 계단에 발을 올려 내디디려다 말고, 내려디뎠다. 빌라 입구에 서서 목을 빼고 골목을 내다보았다. 진홍슈퍼 간판 불빛과 전봇대에 설치해 놓은 가로등 불빛으로 인해 골목은 아주 어둡지는 않았다. 누군가 골목을 걸어 올라오고 있었다. 노인인가 했는데, 교복 차림의 남학생이었다. 남학생은 빌라를 지나쳐갔다. 셔터 내리는 소리가 들려오더니 진홍슈퍼 간판 불빛이 꺼졌다. 그녀는 망설이다가 골목을 걸어 내려갔다.

발이 부은 탓에 슬리퍼를 헐떡헐떡 끌면서 골목을 헤

"The money she's borrowed?"

All of a sudden, she felt that she had to have the money back from the man even if his wife was not home yet. She just had to have the money that night no matter what.

"My father-in-law said that he'd lent your wife 300,000 *won*. I was told your wife would return it to me. I've been waiting and waiting..."

"That's impossible! She wouldn't borrow money from other people that easily," he interrupted her.

"Is she still not back?"

"My wife couldn't have borrowed any money..." he tilted his head in disbelief.

"My father-in-law told me that the lady living in Unit 202 borrowed 300,000 *won*... she still is..."

"My wife..."

The man seemed embarrassed at first, but then he tensed up when he heard a little girl calling him quietly from behind.

"Daddy..."

"My wife..." he said again.

The man shut his mouth and then sighed for a moment. He stared at her for a couple of seconds and then finally closed the door.

"Excuse me..."

매는데, 어느 집 대문 앞에 내놓은 장롱이 그녀의 눈에 들어왔다. 자개장롱이었다. 퍼즐처럼 이어붙인 자개들이 어둠 속에서 야릇한 빛깔을 발산하고 있었다. 그녀는 그 빛에 홀리기라도 한 듯 장롱 가까이 다가갔다.

노인이 혹 저 자개장롱 안에 들어가 잠들어 있는 건 아닐까. 자신이 주운 자개장롱을 다른 누군가가 주워가기라도 할까 봐 그 안에 들어가 웅크려 있다 깜박 잠든 게 아닐까.

그녀는 한 발짝 더 자개장롱에 다가섰다. 자개장롱 문 손잡이를 움켜쥐었다. 한순간 숨을 멈추고 자개장롱 문을 활짝 열어젖혔다.

자개장롱 속은 그러나 텅 비어 있었다. 그녀 자신이라도 들어가 웅크려 잠들고 싶은 충동이 들만큼 텅……

그녀는 그 텅 빈 공간을 응시하면서 느닷없이 당겨오는 배를 어루만졌다.

She stood in front of the closed door for a while, unable to turn around and leave. What was this? She still wasn't back yet? Was he offended by her visiting this late at night like she was some kind of creditor? She wouldn't borrow money that easily? Does that mean the old man tricked me? When on earth were they going to come home? Why weren't they home already?'

She was about to climb up the stairs, but she changed her mind and climbed down the stairs instead. As she stood at the entrance to the condo complex, she craned her neck to look up the alley. The alley was not that dark thanks to the neon sign of Chin-hung Mart and a street light on top of an electric pole. Someone was walking up the alley. At first, she thought it was the old man, but soon saw it was a male student passing by. She heard shutters coming down and the neon sign of the mart went out. She hesitated a bit, and then began to walk down the alley.

She wandered along the alley in the scuffs she was wearing because of her swollen feet. She suddenly spotted a wardrobe in front of a house. It was a wardrobe inlaid with mother-of-pearl. The

5

그녀는 또다시 노인의 방에 들어와 있었다. 방 안을 한 번 둘러본 뒤 책상으로 가서 앉았다. 책상에 바짝 몸을 당겨 앉고 볼펜을 집어 들었다. '르'라는 글자 위에 볼펜 촉을 가져다댔다. 습자지가 그 위에 덧대어져 있기라도 한 듯 똑같이 '르'를 그려나갔다. 덧쓴 꼴이 되어 '르'는 다른 글자보다 굵고 진해져서는, 유별나게 튀어 보였다. 그녀는 '르' 다음에 줄줄이 이어져 나오는 글자들도 똑같이 그려나갔다.

르비딤에서 발행하여 시내 광야에 진쳤고 시내 광야에서 발행하여 기브롯핫다아와에 진쳤고 기브롯핫다아와에서 발행하여 하세롯에 진쳤고 하세롯에서 발행하여 릿마에 진쳤고 릿마에서 발행하여 림몬베레스에 진쳤고 림몬베

설마 저 장롱 속에 들어가 있는 건 아닐 테지…….

mother-of-pearl pieces on its surface, put together like in a puzzle, reflected all sorts of odd colors.
As if drawn to the wardrobe's dazzling colors, she
walked up to it.

Was the old man sleeping inside this wardrobe?
Suppose he wanted the wardrobe for himself and
decided to sit inside to keep it from being taken
away by somebody else, only to fall asleep there.

She took another step toward the wardrobe and
grabbed the door handle. Holding her breath, she
flung the door wide open.

But it was empty—so hollow that she wanted to
crawl in and sleep there herself.

She stared at the empty space, stroking her belly
that had started to tighten again all of a sudden.

5

She was back in the old man's room. As she
looked around the room, she decided to finally
walk up to the desk and sit down on his chair. She
picked up a ball-point pen and put the tip down
on the letter R and began tracing along its lines as
if there was a piece of writing paper placed on the
page so that she could copy what was on the page.

그녀는 문득 노인이 장롱 속에 숨어 있을 것만 같은 생각이 들었다. 노인이 주워 모은 고물들 속에 숨어 혼몽에 취해 있을 것만 같은……. 그녀는 장롱 쪽으로 조심스럽게 다가갔다.

설마…….

그녀는 그러면서도 기어이 장롱 손잡이로 손을 뻗었다. 손잡이를 슬쩍 움켜잡았다. 덜커덕 소리가 나도록 장롱 문을 열었다. 주저하면서도 황급히 장롱 속을 살피던 그녀는 깜짝 놀랐다. 고물들로 꽉 차 있어야 할 장롱 속이 텅 비어 있었던 것이다. 골목에 내놓아져 있던 자개장롱과 마찬가지로. 순간적으로 장롱 속 텅 빈 공간과 자개장롱 속 텅 빈 공간이 오버랩 되면서, 그녀는 그 텅 빈 공간으로 빨려 들어가는 것만 같은 현기증을 느꼈다.

노인네가 고물들을 다 어디다 치운 것일까. 전날 저녁에도 노인네는 밥솥을 주워오지 않았던가. 흘끔흘끔 내 눈치를 살피며 얼른 방으로 가지고 들어가지 않았던가. 그녀는 장롱 문을 도로 꼭 닫았다. 다시 책상으로 가서 앉았다.

노트를 넘기던 그녀의 손이 머뭇머뭇하더니 멈췄다.

In fact, she was writing over the letter R, the letter looked thicker and stood out among the letters on the page. She kept tracing on other letters, line by line.

And they departed from Rephidim, and pitched in the wilderness of Sinai. And they removed from the desert of Sinai, and pitched at Kibroth-hattaavah. And they departed from Kibroth-hattaavah, and encamped at Hazeroth. And they departed from Hazeroth, and pitched in Rithmah. And they departed from Rithmah, and pitched at Rimmon-parez. And they departed from Rimmon-parez

He couldn't have been inside that wardrobe, could he have been?

She was now convinced that the old man was hiding inside the wardrobe in the room, in some sort of delirium. She inched carefully towards this wardrobe.

"It can't be..."

Nevertheless, she reached for the door handle. She grabbed the handle and pulled hard. The door opened with a big clunk. She poked her head inside and her eyes widened. The wardrobe was empty. It was supposed to be packed with the junk

그녀의 눈동자가 글자들을 훑어 내려갔다.

셈의 족보는 이러하다. 셈은 나이가 백 세 되었을 때, 아르팍삿을 낳았다…… 아르팍삿은 삼십오 세에 셀라흐를 낳았다…… 셀라흐는 삼십 세에 에베르를 낳았다. 에베르를 낳은 뒤,

의식하지 못하는 사이에, 그녀의 손이 볼펜을 집어 들었다. 손등의 심줄들이 불거지도록 힘을 주어 글자 위에 글자를 덧그려 나가기 시작했다.

낳았다

낳은 뒤,

the old man had brought home from the alleys. Instantly, in her mind, the empty space inside the wardrobe converged with the hollow interior of the mother-of-pearl wardrobe back in the alley. She was overwhelmed by vertigo so severe that she felt she was being violently pulled back into the hollowness of the wardrobes.

Where had he put away all the junk? He brought home a rice cooker only the evening before. He had hurried it into his room, stealing glances at her. She closed the wardrobe door tightly and went back to the desk and sat down on the chair again.

She began flipping through the pages and then on one page, she hesitated, but soon started reading it through.

These are the generations of Shem: Shem was an hundred years old, and begat Arphaxad... And Arphaxad lived five and thirty years, and begat Salah... And Salah lived thirty years, and begat Eber: And Salah lived after he begat Eber,

Unconsciously, her hand grabbed the ballpoint pen and began overwriting the letters on the page, pressing the pen so hard that the veins on the back

어느 순간 마비되듯, 볼펜을 움켜잡은 손의 움직임을 멈추었다. 너무 꽉 누르고 있어서인지, 볼펜에서 잉크가 흘러나와 검은 웅덩이를 만들었다. 웅덩이는 점점 넓고 짙어졌고, 웅덩이 속으로 글자들이 수몰되듯 빨려 들어갔다.

낳고 또 낳아 동아줄처럼 질긴 족보로 이어져 내려온 사람들이 야밤(夜—)처럼 검은 웅덩이 속으로 수장되고 있었다.

그녀는 웅덩이를 넓히기라도 하듯 둥그렇게 원을 그렸다. 노트 위의 글자들이 한 글자도 빠뜨림 없이 웅덩이 속으로 빨려 들어갈 때까지 기다리다 한순간 몸을 일으켰다.

노인도, 남편도 돌아오지 않고 있었다.

그리고 202호 여자도.

6

들통 속 오리뼈 국물은 바닥까지 졸아들어 있었다. 한 국자도 못 되게 졸아든 국물 속에서 뼈들이 악다구니를 쳐댔다. 그녀는 가스레인지 불을 한껏 올렸다. 가스레

of her hand bulged out.

begat

after he begat

At one point, the hand she held the pen with stopped altogether as if it had suffered sudden paralysis. Perhaps she'd been pressing the pen down too hard. The pen started leaking. Soon the ink from the pen made a dark pool on the page. As the pool became larger and darker, the letters on the page were sucked into it.

All those people who were begotten by the begotten along the tenacious line of their genealogy were drowning in the pool as dark as the darkest night.

She drew circles as if to enlarge the pool. She waited until the pool sucked in all the letters on the page, leaving no letter untouched. Then she stood up.

Neither the old man nor her husband was back home.

Nor was the woman in Unit 202.

인지 불이 허기진 날짐승의 혀처럼 들통 바닥을 핥아댔다. 국물이 졸아들어 뼈들밖에는 남지 않을 때까지 그녀는 꼼짝 않고 지키고 서 있었다. 그녀의 얼굴과 목은 열기를 견디느라 땀으로 번들거렸다. 국물이 졸아들다 못해 뼈들이 허옇게 말라갔다.

오늘 밤 노인은 한 숟가락의 오리 뼈 국물도 목구멍으로 흘려 넣지 못하리라.

그녀는 뚜껑을 꼭 닫고 가스레인지 불을 껐다. 밤새 틀어놓는다 해도 오리 뼈 고는 냄새가 뿌리 뽑히지 못하리라는 걸 알지만 환풍기를 틀었다.

그녀는 노인의 영정사진을 한 번 바라본 뒤 현관문 쪽으로 걸어갔다. 빌라 계단을 내려가 골목으로 들어섰다. 골목에서 길을 잃었을지도 모르는 노인을 찾기 위해. 그녀가 노인을 찾아 집에 돌아왔을 때, 남편과 202호 여자가 돌아와 있기를 바라며. 정말이지 아무렇지도 않게.

『제35회 이상문학상 작품집』, 문학사상, 2011

6

The duck-bone broth in the big pot had reduced to the very dregs of the pot. Inside the remaining ladleful of broth, the bones brawled and clattered madly. She turned the heat to full. The tongues of fire licked the bottom of the pot, like hungry fowls coming down upon it. She stood still by the pot waiting for the broth to dwindle to nothing, leaving nothing but the bones dry. Her face and neck were glossy with sweat. There was hardly any broth left in the pot and the bones had dried white.

"Tonight, the old man won't be able to put even a single spoon of duck-bone broth down his gullet."

She put the lid on the pot tightly and turned off the heat. She knew that she could never drive the stench of boiled duck bones completely out of her place even if she kept the ventilation fan on all night. Despite it all, she did switch the ventilation fan on.

She took a look at the old man's funeral-portrait and walked towards the front door. She went down the stairs into the alley to look for the old man. He might have gotten lost in the alleys. She hoped that by the time she returned home with the old man, her husband and the woman living in Unit 202 would be back, as if nothing had happened.

* English translation first published in the quarterly *ASIA*, No. 18.

Translated by Jeon Miseli

해설

Afterword

검은 웅덩이를 닮은 밤

고봉준 (문학평론가)

김숨의 문장들은 느리다. 그녀의 소설들은 낮고 음울한 소리로 연결된 음악처럼 삶의 저층에 쌓여 있는 어두운 시간들을 천천히 재생한다. 이 독특한 분위기는 그녀 특유의 섬세한 묘사와 결합하여 읽는 사람들에게 불편한 느낌을 준다. 이러한 묘사의 방식을 그로테스크하다고 말한다면 김숨의 문장, 특히 묘사들은 그로테스크하다고 평가할 수도 있다. 하지만 다른 작가들의 그로테스크한 묘사와 달리 김숨의 그것은 어떤 경우에도 담담한 어조를 벗어나지 않는다. 대상을 심하게 왜곡하는 과장적인 표현법이 어떠한 심적 미동도 허락되지 않는 고요함과 나란하게 놓이는 세계, 이것이 김숨 소설

Night Like A Black Puddle

Ko Bong-jun (literary critic)

Kim Soom's sentences have a leisurely pace. Like music that consists of low, gloomy melodies, it slowly plays the dark times that accumulate in the far recesses of our lives. This unique atmosphere combined with Kim Soom's characteristically delicate portrayals give readers a feeling of discomfort. If one refers to this style as "grotesque," one could say that Kim Soom writes grotesque sentences and depictions. But unlike the "grotesqueness" we see in works of other writers, Kim Soom's grotesque never strays from its unemotional tone. A world in which hyperbolic expressions that distort characters are juxtaposed against a stillness that does not

의 불편한 특징이다.

「아무도 돌아오지 않는 밤」에서 이 불편함을 환기하는 대상은 시아버지와, 집 안을 노린내로 채우는 구릿빛 양은들통 속의 '오리 뼈'이다. 소설의 내용은 이렇다. 화자 '나'는 전세로 얻은 빌라에서 남편과 함께 살고 있다. 하지만 그들의 빌라에는 불편한 동거인, 즉 시아버지가 함께 살고 있다. 임신 7개월에 접어든 '나'가 시아버지와 함께 사는 이유는 남편이 시아버지의 빌라를 주식과 펀드로 날려버렸기 때문이다. 이들 세 사람의 동거는 결코 순탄하지 않다. 이들 부부와 시아버지 모두가 동거를 원하지 않는다. 시아버지는 아들에게 자신의 빌라를 처분한 돈을 받아 실버타운에 입주하기를 원한다. 하지만 아들 부부에게는 그만한 돈이 없다. 시아버지가 돈을 요구한 뒤로 남편은 의도적으로 귀가 시간을 늦추었다. 그래서 임신 때문에 집 바깥으로 나가지 못하는 '나'와 시아버지가 302호에서 함께 보내게 된다. 다행히 시아버지는 아침부터 저녁까지, 그러니까 하루의 대부분을 집 밖에서 보낸다. 대신 그는 자신의 분신 같은 존재를 집 안에 남겨둔다. 오리 뼈가 담겨 있는 양은들통이 그것이다. 들통 속의 오리 뼈는 특유의 노린내

allow the least bit of emotion—this is the discomfiting characteristic of Kim Soom's fiction.

In "The Night Nobody Returns Home," the source of this discomfort is the protagonist's father-in-law and the duck bones in the copper-colored nickel silver pot fill the house with stench. The premise of the story is as follows: Yeong-suk the protagonist lives in a rented apartment with her husband. But they also live with a dependent who makes live uncomfortable for them—Yeong-suk's father-in-law. The reason Yeong-suk, who is seven months into her pregnancy, must live with her father-in-law is because her husband lost the father-in-law's house in a bad investment. Their cohabitation is not easy. No one likes this arrangement. The father-in-law wants to use the money he got from selling his place to get himself a place at an old folks' village. But the couple doesn't not have that kind of money. Once the father-in-law starts demanding the money, the husband begins to come home from work later. And so Yeong-suk, who has a hard time leaving the apartment because of her pregnancy, is trapped in apartment Unit 302 with her father-in-law. Thankfully, the father-in-law spends most of the day outside, but he leaves

를 풍기면서 집 전체를 점령해버린다.

이 소설에서 시아버지와 그가 집 바깥에서 가지고 들어오는 출처를 알 수 없는 '오리 뼈'는 타자성의 상징이다. 그것은 '나'가 감당할 수 없는, 그렇지만 감당하지 않을 수도 없는 것들이다. 소설은 시아버지와 그가 고는 '오리 뼈'에 대한 '나'의 심적 태도를 묘사하는 데 상당한 지면을 할애하고 있다. 사실상 '나'는 시아버지라는 존재 자체가 못마땅하다. 때문에 이 소설에서 시아버지, 노린내를 풍기는 오리 뼈, 시아버지가 주워오는 고물들은 일종의 비존재, 즉 타자의 형상들이며, 시아버지의 공간은 텅 빈 장롱 속의 "검은 웅덩이"나 거실에 걸려 있는 '영정사진'처럼 죽음을 암시한다. 그것들은 출산(생명)을 앞두고 있는 '나'와 동일한 세계에 거주할 수 있는 것들이 아니다. 그래서 소설의 전반부는 생명과 죽음, 주체와 타자의 경계를 지켜내려는 '나'의 고투가 중심을 이룬다. '나'에게 노인은 "뭉그러진 빨랫비누 같은 얼굴", "낯설고 이상한 공포심"의 세계일 뿐이다. "오리 뼈 곤 국물을 하도 먹어대서인지 노인의 얼굴에 부옇게 살이 오르는 동안, 그녀는 쇠꼬챙이처럼 말라갔다"라는 진술은 생명과 죽음, 존재와 타자의 비대칭성을 의미한다.

his stand-in, the copper-colored nickel silver pot containing duck bones, at home. The duck bones take over the house with its unique stench.

The father-in-law and the duck bones of unknown origin serve as the symbol of "the other." It is too much for Yeong-suk to bear, but it does not need to be tolerated if she chose not to. The story devotes a great deal of focus on describing the father-in-law and the psychological reaction of the protagonist to the duck bone broth that he makes. In truth, Yeong-suk begrudges the father-in-law's existence. This is reflected in the fact that the father-in-law, the foul-smelling duck bones, and the junk that he finds outside and brings home are all images of a non-being, or "the other" and the spaces that he occupy, such as the "dark pool" inside the father-in-law's empty wardrobe or the funeral portrait hanging on the living room wall, foreshadow death. These are not things that can coexist in the world with Yeong-suk, who is about to make life by giving birth. And so the first part of the story is centered around Yeong-suk's struggle as she tries to defend the boundary between life and death, and ego and "the other." To her, the old man is a "face that looked like a crumbling bar of

소설의 중반부에서 이 경계는 '30만 원'이라는 화폐적 가치에 의해 관통된다. 시아버지가 자신이 아래층 여자에게 빌려준 돈을 '나'에게 갚으라고 했다는 사실을 알려주면서 상황은 전혀 다른 방향으로 흘러간다. 자신의 의지와 상관없이 채권자가 된 '나'는 같은 빌라에 살면서도 전혀 알지 못했던 202호 여자의 귀가에 관심을 쏟기 시작한다. 물론 '나'가 기다리는 것은 여자가 아니라 '돈'이지만, 이 사건을 계기로 '나'와 타자들의 관계가 일변한 것은 분명하다. 먼저 '나'는 아무리 기다려도 돌아오지 않는 2층 여자를 기다리다가 빌라 전체에 불이 켜진 창문이 없다는 사실을 알게 된다. 이 장면은 '나'의 고립감을 비현실적인 장면으로 묘사함으로써 인간의 내면에 잠재되어 있는 근원적인 불안과 공포의 심리를 드러내는 듯하다. 하지만 이 작품의 중심은 불안과 공포가 아니라 생명과 죽음, 존재와 타자의 관계이다. 그래서 시아버지를 포함해 남편, 202호 여자에 대한 '나'의 태도 변화는 흥미롭다. 처음에 '나'는 시아버지가 자신의 세계에서 사라지기를 간절히 바랐다. 만일 이들 부부에게 돈이 있었다면 '나'의 바람은 쉽게 이루어졌을 것이다. 하지만 소설이 중반을 지나면서 '나'의 마음속

washing soap" or an "unfamiliar and inexplicable fear." The depiction, "As the old man's face got fleshy, perhaps thanks to the duck-bone soup, she became as thin as an iron skewer" attests to the asymmetry of life and death, self and the other.

In the middle part of the story, this boundary is transected by a monetary value of 300,000 *won*. The story starts to run in a completely new direction when the father-in-law informs her that the woman who lives downstairs owes him 300,000 and that he told the woman to give the money to Yeong-suk. Now an unwitting creditor, Yeong-suk begins to take a great deal of interest in when the woman who lives in apartment unit 202 comes home from work, a woman she had never met before even though they lived in the same building. Of course, it is the money, not the woman, that Yeong-suk is interested in, but it is certain that the relationship between Yeong-suk and "the others" shift through this new development. Yeong-suk waits and waits for the woman in unit 202 until she discovers one day that there isn't a single house in the apartment building with the light on. This scene seems to reveal the fundamental and latent anxiety and fear of human beings through a surreal depic-

에선 밤 11시가 다 되도록 돌아오지 않는 노인을 걱정하는 마음과 노인이 돌아오고 있지 않는 것에 대한 안도의 마음이 교차하기 시작한다. 또한 '나'는 빌라의 현관문이 열리고 닫히는 소리에 예민하게 반응하고, 심지어 두 번이나 찾아갈 정도로 202호 여자의 귀가를 애타게 기다리게 된다. 이러한 '나'의 간절한 기다림에도 불구하고 돌아와야 할 사람들 가운데 누구도 돌아오지 않는 것이 소설의 상황이다. "노인도, 남편도 돌아오지 않고 있었다. 그리고 202호 여자도." 기다리지 않아도 때가 되면 돌아오던 것들을 간절하게 기다리기 시작하면서 돌아오지 않는다는 것은 얼마나 큰 아이러니인가. 이 간절한 기다림의 층위에서 노인, 남편, 여자는 동일한 의미를 부여받는다. 그리고 마지막 장면에서 '나'는 마침내 그들을 찾아 집을 나선다. "골목에서 길을 잃었을지도 모르는 노인을 찾기 위해"서가 이유이다. 하지만 우리는 안다. 노인이 골목에서 길을 잃는 일이 발생할 수 없다는 것을. 그리고 '나'는 기원한다. "그녀가 노인을 찾아 집에 돌아왔을 때, 남편과 202호 여자가 돌아와 있기를." 어느 순간 '나'는 처음과 달리 그들 모두가 무사히 귀가하기를 바라고 있다. 바로 이 지점에서 생

tion of Yeong-suk's sense of isolation. However, the focus of this work is not anxiety and fear, but the relationship between the self and the other. The change of attitude we see in Yeong-suk in her perspective of her father-in-law, and even her husband and the woman in unit 202 is interesting. At first, Yeong-suk desperately wanted her father-in-law to disappear from her world. If the couple had had money, this would have been easily accomplished. But around halfway through the story, Yeong-suk's concern for the old man who does not return home when it's nearly eleven at night intersects with her hopes that he may not return. Also, Yeong-suk becomes very sensitive to the sounds of apartment doors opening and closing, and desperately awaits the return of the woman in unit 202, so much so that she knocks on her door twice. The situation in the story is that, despite the protagonist's earnest waiting, no one has shown up yet. "It was past ten and the old man was not back home yet. Her husband and the woman in Unit 202 weren't back, either." What a great irony that the unwelcome people who always returned home on time should be late the moment she eagerly wishes their return! In this earnest wait, the old man, the

명과 죽음, 주체와 타자의 경계는 심각하게 관통된다. "낳고 또 낳아 동아줄처럼 질긴 족보로 이어져 내려온 사람들이 야밤처럼 검은 웅덩이 속으로 수장되고 있었다"라는 문장이 그것이다. 이 문장에서 '족보'는 죽음과 삶이 단절되는 방식으로 연속되는 시간의 계기를 의미한다. '나'는 삶과 죽음 모두가 검은 웅덩이 속으로 수장되는 장면을 회피하지 않고 "웅덩이를 넓히기라도 하듯 둥그렇게 원"을 그린다. 이것은 생명과 주체의 세계가 죽음과 타자에 의해 관통되었다는 것을 가리킨다. 경계가 사라질 때, 모든 것들은 불투명해진다. 검은 웅덩이를 닮은 밤처럼.

husband, and the woman in unit 202 are given equal meaning. And in the last scene, Yeong-suk finally sets out to look for them. It is to find the "old man who might have gotten lost in the alleys." But we cannot be fooled. We know that there is no chance that the old man has lost his way in the alleys. And Yeong-suk hopes that "by the time she came home with the old man, her husband and the woman living in Unit 202 would have been back already." Unlike when the story began, the protagonist finds herself wishing for their safe return. At this very point, the boundary between life and death, and the self and the other is profoundly transected. The sentence, "All those people who were begotten by the begotten along the tenacious line of their genealogy were drowning in the pool as dark as the darkest night" refers to genealogy as a stretch of time that is a series of death separated from life. Instead of looking away from the vision of both life and death drowning in the "dark pool," she draws "circles as if to enlarge the pool." This signifies that the world of life and the self has been transected by the world of death and the other. When the boundary dissolves, everything becomes unclear. Like the night as dark as the black pool.

비평의 목소리

Critical Acclaim

환상과 마법조차도 현실의 감금을 환기하는 저주에 불과할 때, 김숨이 직조해낸 그로테스크한 현실의 이미지는 말 그대로 '봉인', 그 자체라고 할 수 있다. 김숨의 소설 어디를 뒤진다 해도 존재의 음화라고 할 수 있을 잔혹한 삶의 이미지와 조우하게 된다. 이 잔혹하고 그로테스크한 상황과 공간의 이미지는 독자의 이성보다 먼저 신경과 심장을 각성시킨다. 이는 한편 김숨의 소설적 성과가 동시대 문화의 키워드로 부상한 '감각성'과의 차별성에서 비롯된다는 말이기도 하다. 악취와 어둠이 가득 찬 김숨의 공간들은 우리의 삶이 은폐하고 있는 심연을 아프고 깊게 각인하는 미학적 기획으로 다가

At a time when even fantasies and magic remind us of our *confinement* to reality, the grotesque reality that Kim Soom weaves *encase* us to reality. No matter where you go in the world of Kim Soom's fiction, you will come face to face with the images of the cruelty of life that could be considered the film negative of existence. The images of these grotesque situations and spaces alert the reader's nerves and heart before it surfaces on the level of reason. Perhaps this is another way of saying that Kim Soom's accomplishments as a writer is distinct from the "sensuality" that has become the cultural keyword of her contemporaries. Kim Soom's spac-

온다.

강유정

김숨의 소설은 연극적이다. 작위적이라는 말이 아니라 그저 재연이 쉽다는 말이다. 가독성 높은 흥미로운 사건도, 인물들 간의 실감 나는 대화도, 현실과 밀착된 공간도 부재하지만, 그 때문에 오히려 김숨 소설은 연극에 알맞다. "다섯 발짝"의 공간을 통한 시간의 압축, 주로 독백에 가까운 대화, 서로의 동선을 맞추는 리허설을 필요치 않는 반복적 행위, 한 편의 연극마다 그저 침대, 책상, 식탁, 항아리가 전부일 뿐인 간소한 소품, 세 가지 색만을 허용하는 무대. 이처럼 단조로운 김숨의 극본이 만들어내는 한 편의 연극은 그야말로 한 인생의 숨이 완전히 끊어지는 과정, 완벽히 소실되는 과정 바로 그것이다. (……) 김숨의 연극은 반복되는 임종의 순간이자 거대한 장례식인 것이다. 반복은 습관을 만들어내고 습관은 두려움을 없앤다. 홀로 남겨짐에 대한 공포로 인해 쓰게 되었다(「작가의 말」)는 몇 편의 소설은 이렇게 반복을 통해 영원한 고립인 죽음에 대한 두려움을 휘발시킨다. 김숨의 반복강박은 미래완료형의

es, filled with stench and darkness, is a aesthetic design that touches on the concealed undercurrents of life in a painful, profound way.

Kang Yu-jeong

Kim Soom's stories are theatrical. This does not mean they come off as artificial, but simply that it is easy to reproduce. Her stories have no gripping plots we see in page-turners, no life-like dialogue between characters, and no spaces grounded in reality, but these factors make Kim Soom's stories suitable for the stage—compression of time through the space of pentameters, conversations that are usually like monologues, and repetitive actions that do not require rehearsals to determine blockings, simple props and set of a bed, a desk, a table, and a jar for every play, and a color palette of just three colors. Such simple plays derived from Kim Soom's stories is the process through which the breath on one life is completely snuffed and absolutely eliminated... [...] Kim Soom's play is a continuous replay of the moment of death and a massive funeral. The repetition creates habit and habit in turn eliminates fear. In a few stories that were inspired by "the terror of being left all alone

사건을 현재진행형으로 되풀이하면서 감정의 경계를 성취한다.

조연정

쇠못에 찔리고 망치에 찧이고 노동을 박탈당하고 녹에 부식되면서 사라져간 자들을 상기하고자 할 때, 우리는 그들을 동경하고 싶은 것인가, 찬양하고 싶은 것인가, 아니면 위로하고 싶은 것인가. 김숨 식의 독특함은 그 세대로 (과거로) 되돌아가는 것이 아니라, 그 세대를 지금(현재)으로 끌어당긴다. 어떤 식이냐 하면, 지난 세대라는 박제된 대상을 생생한 세목을 거느린 현실로 재생시켜 과거를 기리는 것이 아니라, 거꾸로, 생생했었을 과거를 물화된 정물의 윤곽으로 새겨 현실에 봉헌하는 것이다. 정물인 삶이 어디 있으랴. 스스로 호출해낸 삶을 정물처럼 그리는 것은 쉬운 기교가 아니다. 김숨이 그것을 해낸 수법은 서로에게 제한적인 시선만 허용하고 인물의 안쪽으로 들어가지 않는 것이었다. 그는 개인의 표정이나 절규를 동원하는 것은 쉬운 연민을 소진시키게 될지도 모른다는 것을 알고 있다. 집단의 동요와 실루엣이 굵직하게 새겨질 때 잔혹한 연민은 쉽게

(From the author's note)," the fear of death as an eternal isolation evaporates through this process of repetition. Kim Soom's obsession with repetition builds a boundary of emotions by repeating an event in the future perfect tense in the present continuous tense.

Jo Yeon-jeong

When we wish to remember those who were stabbed by iron nails, hit by hammers, and stripped of their labor until they rusted away and disappeared, do we mean to admire them or praise them? Or to comfort their souls? Kim Soom's uniqueness lies in that she pulls the generation to the present setting rather than returning to the past. For example, rather than commemorating the past by bringing a taxidermy subject back to life and placing it back in a reality with vivid details, she turns a vivid past into an outline of a still life and dedicating it to reality. No life is an object in a painting. It is no easy task for a writer to take a life she conjured up herself and paint it like an object. Kim Soom accomplishes this by adhering to limited views and not going inside the head of her characters. She knows that depictions of individuals' facial

사라지지 않는다. 지난 세대를 불러들인다는 것은 그들을 동정하거나 찬양하려는 게 아니라 그저 위로하고 싶다는 뜻임을 우리는 안다. 잔혹한 연민만이 그것을, 동정도 찬양도 아닌 위로를 감당할 수 있을 것이다. 김숨이 어떤 삶을 체현한 '인물'이 아니라 어떤 삶들을 배출한 '시공(時空)'을 한 편의 수난극으로 제출했을 때, 이것은 누군가를 재현한 것이 아니라 누군가에게 제물처럼 바쳐지는 이야기다. 『철』은 '그들'을 위로하기 위해 김숨이 올린 두 번째 제의극이다.

백지은

유령 같은 존재들의 기이한 말과 행위들이 손쉽게 의미로 치환될 수 없음에도 불구하고 어딘지 모르게 끊임없이 불쾌감과 불안함을 유발할 수 있다는 것을 김숨의 『노란 개를 버리러』는 인상적으로 보여준다. 말하자면 사건과 행위의 층위에서 김숨의 소설은 사실적이라고 할 수는 없으나, 사실(fact) 너머의 리얼리티를 끊임없이 환기하고 있다는 점에서 정신분석학에서 말하는 실재(the real)의 영역에 매우 가까이 근접해 있음을 실연(實演)해 보이는 텍스트라 할 수 있을 것이다. 라캉의 말을

expressions or cries of pain may only inspire cheap pity. Only when the disquiet and silhouette of a group is etched in deep, thick lines can the ruthless sympathy persist. We know that her intention in invoking the past generation is to simply comfort them, not to pity or praise. A ruthless sympathy is perhaps the only way to handle console, not pity or praise. When Kim Soom presents, in the form of a "Passion play," a time and space that gave rise to certain kinds of life rather than characters who have experienced certain lives, the story is not re-played for someone, but offered before someone like a sacrifice. *The Iron* the second "memorial ritual play" Kim Soom offers to console "them."

Baek Ji-eun

In a memorable way, Kim Soom's *To Abandon A Yellow Dog* portrays phantom-like beings and their strange words and actions we cannot swiftly pin a meaning on but continue to inspire discomfort and disquiet we cannot name. In other words, one cannot aruge that Kim Soom's stories are "realistic" on the level of the events or actions that occur, but come very close to the realm of "the real" in the psychoanalytical context by continuously referring

변주하건대, 실로 불안은 독자 자신을 속이지 않는 법이다. 소설 속 인물들이 보여주는 무의미한 대화와 몸짓들이 직접적으로 텍스트 바깥의 구체적 현실을 타격하지는 않는 것처럼 보여도, 이를 읽는 독자가 마치 제발 저리듯 모종의 이물감을 발견하고 섬뜩해하는 것은 바로 이 때문이다. 그렇다면, 이 이물감의 정체는 무엇인가? 인간에게 작용하는 가장 원초적인 불안 요소는 무엇인가? 그것은 바로 삶의 토대로 작용하고 있는 잠재적인 것으로서의 죽음일 것이다.

강동호

to the reality that lies beyond the facts. Building on Lacan, anxiety cannot fool the reader. Even though it appears the meaningless conversations between characters and their gestures are not connect to any specific reality outside the world of the text, the readers make the connection on their own and feel a chill down their spine as they happen upon a sort of discomfort, like a pebble in a shoe. So exactly what is this discomfort? What is the most primal fear that affects human beings? It is perhaps death as a potential that operates on the premise of life.

Kang Dong-ho

김숨

김숨은 1974년 7월 23일 울산 방어진 바닷가 마을에서 태어났다. 걸음과 말을 뗄 때까지 울산현대조선소가 바라다 보이는 마을에서 자랐다. 여섯 살 때 아버지가 중동 근로자가 되어 멀리 떠나게 되자 어머니와 오빠, 남동생과 함께 충남 금산군 추부의 할아버지 집으로 들어가 살게 되었다. 무서움을 유난히 잘 타서 붉은 벼슬을 곧추세운 수탉이 마당을 돌아다니면 마루에서 내려가지 못했다고 한다.

멀리 미루나무가 유령처럼 서 있던 신작로로 흰 상여가 미숫가루 같은 먼지를 일으키면서 지나가던 장면이, 최초로 경험한 죽음의 이미지였다. 쌀겨먼지와 쥐가 들끓는 방앗간에서 숨바꼭질 놀이를 하거나, 논두렁과 밭으로 나물을 뜯으러 다니거나, 뙤약볕이 굵은 소금처럼 내리는 냇가에서 소꿉놀이를 하면서 자랐다. 그 시절 늙고 병든 어른들 틈바구니에서 자라면서 어렴풋이나마 경험한 인생의 희로애락과 죽음, 강렬하게 목격했던 이미지들―쏠개즙처럼 검푸르던 저수지와 동네 총각이

Kim Soom

Kim Soom was born on July 23, 1974 at a seaside village called Bangeojin in Ulsan. Until she learned to talk and walk, she lived in the village that looked out onto the Ulsan Hyundai Shipyard. She went to live at her grandfather's house in Geumsan-gun Chubu in Chungcheongnam-do with her mother and two brothers at the age of seven when her father left to be a laborer in the Middle East. She was easily scared; she couldn't go into the yard when the rooster was strutting about the yard with its comb red and stiff.

A white bier passing down the newly paved road with a ghostly poplar tree in the distance, leaving a flour-like dust in its wake was her first experience with images of death. She grew up playing hide-and-seek in a mill full of rice bran powder and mice, harvesting wild vegetables in the vegetables patches and between rice paddies, or playing house by a brook where sunlight fell like coarse salt. Her experience with the joys, angers, sadness, and pleasures of life and death, albeit vicariously,

맨손으로 닭의 모가지를 비틀어 잡던 장면, 냇가에서 잡아온 붕어의 배를 따고 내장과 부레를 꺼내던 장면 등—이 소설을 쓰는 데 든든하고 근원적인 에너지와 소재, 주제가 되어주고 있다. 추부초등학교에 입학해 일주일 다니다 대전에 있는 초등학교로 전학을 나왔다. 말이 없는데다 잘 웃지 않아 "너 벙어리니?" 하는 소리를 반 친구로부터 듣기도 했다.

고등학교에 입학해 '청운문학회'라는 문학동아리에 가입, 시를 쓰기 시작했다. 시 습작을 하다, 1997년 스물세 살이 되던 해 긴 글이 쓰고 싶어서 쓴 첫 소설 「느림에 대하여」가《대전일보》신춘문예에 당선, 이듬해인 1998년 「중세의 시간」이《문학동네》신인문학상에 당선되면서 본격적으로 소설 쓰기에 몰두하기 시작했다.

대학교 졸업 후 지방 신문사 교열부에서 근무한 경험이 있는데, 그즈음 마침 IMF가 터졌고, 기자들이 해고되는 과정을 지켜본 경험을 바탕으로 단편 「박의 책상」을 쓰기도 했다. 신문사를 그만두고 충남 공주 쪽에 있는 정신지체장애인생활시설에서 6개월 동안 사회복지사로 근무한 경험이 있다. 그때 함께 생활했던 정신지체장애인들의 얼굴은 음화처럼 가슴속에 남아 있다.

by growing up among old, ailing adults and the powerful images she saw—the reservoir in the neighborhood as dark as bile, a village young man twisting a chicken's neck with his bare hands, and seeing a fish gutted and its intestines and swim bladder scraped out—became a trusty source of energy, themes, and topics in her life as a writer. When she transferred to an elementary school in Daejeon after a week in the first grade at Chubu Elementary School, she was so quiet and seldom laughed that one of her classmates asked her if she was a mute.

In high school, she was a member of a literary club called the Cheongun Literary Society, and began to write poems. She wrote poems for years until 1997, when at the age of twenty-three, she wrote her first story, "On Slowness," which won *the Daejeon Ilbo* Spring Literary Contest. In the following year, another story "Time In The Medieval" won the *Munhakdongnae* New Writer Literary Award, launching her writing career.

When she was working at a small newspaper as a proofreader after college, when the financial crisis of 1997 occurred. She wrote "Park's Desk" based on her observation of reporters getting fired. She

등단 7년 만인 2005년 문학동네에서 첫 소설집『투견』을 냈다. 이후 일찌감치 인생의 변두리로 밀려난 무기력한 가장들의 서글픔을 그린 첫 장편소설『백치들』과 조선소 노동자들이 주인공으로 등장하는『철』을 펴냈다. 2012년 주술적인 반복으로 불안의 증상을 그린 장편『노란 개를 버리러』로 허균문학작가상을, 2013년 실존의 고립감과 부조리를 그린「그 밤의 경숙」으로 현대문학상을, 2013년 장편『여인들과 진화하는 적들』로 대산문학상을 수상했다.

quit the newspaper and worked for six months as a social worker at a home for the mentally disabled near Gongju, Chungcheongnam-do. The faces of the clients she lived with are etched in her heart like a film negative.

Her first short story collection, *The Dogfight*, was published by Munhakdongnae in 2005, seven years after her debut. She went on to write her first novel, *The Idiots*, about the sorrows of the powerless heads of households who have been pushed to the margins of life from early on, and *The Iron*, about shipyard laborers. She received the Heo Gyun Literary Writer Award in 2012 with *To Abandon A Yellow Dog*, a novel that depicts symptoms of anxiety through incantation-like repetition, and the *Hyundae Munhak* Literary Award in 2013 with "Gyeongsook That Night," and the Daesan Literary Award in 2013 with *The Women And The Evolving Foes*, a story about the isolation and absurdity of existence.

번역 **전미세리** Translated by Jeon Miseli

한국외국어대학교 동시통역대학원을 졸업한 후, 캐나다 브리티시 컬럼비아 대학교 도서관학, 아시아학과 문학 석사, 동 대학 비교문학과 박사 학위를 취득하고 강사 및 아시아 도서관 사서로 근무했다. 한국국제교류재단 장학금을 지원받았고, 캐나다 연방정부 사회인문과학연구회의 연구비를 지원받았다. 오정희의 단편 「직녀」를 번역했으며 그 밖에 서평, 논문 등을 출판했다.

Jeon Miseli is graduate from the Graduate School of Simultaneous Interpretation, Hankuk University of Foreign Studies and received her M.L.S. (School of Library and Archival Science), M.A. (Dept. of Asian Studies) and Ph.D. (Programme of Comparative Literature) at the University of British Columbia, Canada. She taught as an instructor in the Dept. of Asian Studies and worked as a reference librarian at the Asian Library, UBC. She was awarded the Korea Foundation Scholarship for Graduate Students in 2000. Her publications include the translation "Weaver Woman"(*Acta Koreana*, Vol. 6, No. 2, July 2003) from the original short story "Chingnyeo"(1970) written by Oh Jung-hee.

감수 **전승희, 데이비드 윌리엄 홍**
Edited by Jeon Seung-hee and David William Hong

전승희는 서울대학교와 하버드대학교에서 영문학과 비교문학으로 박사 학위를 받았으며, 현재 하버드대학교 한국학 연구소의 연구원으로 재직하며 아시아 문예 계간지 《ASIA》 편집위원으로 활동 중이다. 현대 한국문학 및 세계문학을 다룬 논문을 다수 발표했으며, 바흐친의 『장편소설과 민중언어』, 제인 오스틴의 『오만과 편견』 등을 공역했다. 1988년 한국여성연구소의 창립과 《여성과 사회》의 창간에 참여했고, 2002년부터 보스턴 지역 피학대 여성을 위한 단체인 '트랜지션하우스' 운영에 참여해 왔다. 2006년 하버드대학교 한국학 연구소에서 '한국 현대사와 기억'을 주제로 한 워크숍을 주관했다.

Jeon Seung-hee is a member of the Editorial Board of *ASIA*, and a Fellow at the Korea Institute, Harvard University. She received a Ph.D. in English Literature from Seoul National University and a Ph.D. in Comparative Literature from Harvard University. She has presented and published numerous papers on modern Korean and world literature. She is also a co-translator of Mikhail Bakhtin's *Novel and the People's Culture* and Jane Austen's *Pride and Prejudice*. She is a founding member of the Korean Women's Studies Institute and of the biannual Women's Studies' journal *Women and Society* (1988), and she has been working at 'Transition House,' the first and oldest shelter for battered women in New England. She organized a workshop entitled "The Politics of Memory in Modern Korea" at the Korea Institute, Harvard University, in 2006. She also served as an advising committee member for the Asia-Africa Literature Festival in 2007 and for the POSCO Asian Literature Forum in 2008.

데이비드 윌리엄 홍은 미국 일리노이주 시카고에서 태어났다. 일리노이대학교에서 영문학을, 뉴욕대학교에서 영어교육을 공부했다. 지난 2년간 서울에 거주하면서 처음으로 한국인과 아시아계 미국인 문학에 깊이 몰두할 기회를 가졌다. 현재 뉴욕에서 거주하며 강의와 저술 활동을 한다.

David William Hong was born in 1986 in Chicago, Illinois. He studied English Literature at the University of Illinois and English Education at New York University. For the past two years, he lived in Seoul, South Korea, where he was able to immerse himself in Korean and Asian-American literature for the first time. Currently, he lives in New York City, teaching and writing.

바이링궐 에디션 한국 대표 소설 073

아무도 돌아오지 않는 밤

2014년 6월 6일 초판 1쇄 인쇄 | 2014년 6월 13일 초판 1쇄 발행

지은이 김숨 | 옮긴이 전미세리 | 펴낸이 김재범
감수 전승희, 데이비드 윌리엄 홍 | 기획 정은경, 전성태, 이경재
편집 정수인, 이은혜 | 관리 박신영 | 디자인 이춘희
펴낸곳 (주)아시아 | 출판등록 2006년 1월 27일 제406-2006-000004호
주소 서울특별시 동작구 서달로 161-1(흑석동 100-16)
전화 02.821.5055 | 팩스 02.821.5057 | 홈페이지 www.bookasia.org
ISBN 979-11-5662-018-1 (set) | 979-11-5662-035-8 (04810)
값은 뒤표지에 있습니다.

Bi-lingual Edition Modern Korean Literature 073

The Night Nobody Returns Home

Written by Kim Soom I **Translated by** Jeon Miseli
Published by Asia Publishers I 161-1, Seodal-ro, Dongjak-gu, Seoul, Korea
Homepage Address www.bookasia.org I **Tel**. (822).821.5055 I **Fax**. (822).821.5057
First published in Korea by Asia Publishers 2014
ISBN 979-11-5662-018-1 (set) | 979-11-5662-035-8 (04810)

〈바이링궐 에디션 한국 대표 소설〉 작품 목록(1~60)

아시아는 지난 반세기 동안 한국에서 나온 가장 중요하고 첨예한 문제의식을 가진 작가들의 작품들을 선별하여 총 105권의 시리즈를 기획하였다. 하버드 한국학 연구원 및 세계 각국의 우수한 번역진들이 참여하여 외국인들이 읽어도 어색함이 느껴지지 않는 손색없는 번역으로 인정받았다. 이 시리즈는 세계인들에게 문학 한류의 지속적인 힘과 가능성을 입증하는 전집이 될 것이다.

바이링궐 에디션 한국 대표 소설 set 1

분단 Division

산업화 Industrialization

여성 Women

바이링궐 에디션 한국 대표 소설 set 2

자유 Liberty

바이링궐 에디션 한국 대표 소설 set 4

디아스포라 Diaspora

가족 Family

유머 Humor